Pen-Ultimate:

A Speculative Fiction Anthology

Edited by
LJ Cohen and Talib S. Hussain

!?*Interrobang Books*

Pen-Ultimate: A Speculative Fiction Anthology

edited by LJ Cohen and Talib S. Hussain

Published by Interrobang Books
Newton, MA

First print edition: July 2013

ISBN-13: 978-0984787029
ISBN-10: 098478702X

Original cover art and design by Chris Howard
www.saltwaterwitch.com

Contents

Part II: Perception and Transformation

*

Foreword

Writing can often be a pain in the posterior.

First of all, you've got to write stuff, and then write some more. Then you have to have enough confidence to send your work out into the big bad world of publishing markets, only to have it come back to you with nothing more than a form rejection. Your parents, your friends, maybe even your spouse, all encourage you to stop wasting your time on this stuff and go out and get a *real* job, or a *better* job, or at least *some* sort of job where you actually make a decent living.

It can get downright depressing.

What's a writer to do?

You find other people just like you. Other people who want to become writers, or get better at writing. People who will actually sit down and write, and then be brave enough to show their work to other people for *critical review*. In short, you join a writing workshop.

I decided I was going to be a science fiction writer when I was ten years old. I tried to get serious about the writing thing once I finished college. I dutifully finished a story, sent it out, and got it back, over and over. I wondered (as most beginning writers do) if

I was just fooling myself. But I still knew I wanted to be a writer, and was just too stubborn to quit. I found a class taught by SF writer Hal Clement, then got accepted into a small workshop in New York City with Norman Spinrad, Carol Emshwiller and Samuel R. Delany. These people actually saw value in my work, and encouraged me to make it better.

Maybe I would get to be a published writer after all.

I decided that workshopping really helped my fiction, and once I got back to Boston, I found some other like-minded people and formed a science fiction workshop. My writing got more disciplined, my storytelling improved, and within a few months I had written a story which actually sold to a science fiction magazine. A couple of years down the line, a book editor asked me if maybe I had something I could show her. That project sold, and a lot of other stuff sold after that. I credit the encouragement and support of my writing workshop; the group that kept me working on my fiction, and made all of these sales possible.

Fast forward about twenty-five years. I start teaching a writing workshop along with my friend, Jeff Carver. We run half a dozen of these things over the next few years, getting folks to write and workshop. We see a lot of beginning writers get better, and then get better still.

The groups set up workshops of their own, and the writers in those groups start selling stories and novels to major markets. Looking at the quality and variety of the stories in this collection, I expect they will sell a lot more.

We have the proof right here. All the people in this anthology are getting to be damn good writers.

So turn the page, and see just what workshopping can do.

—Craig Shaw Gardner
July 2013

Part I:
Vision and Delusion

In the Shadow of Dyrhólaey

KJ Kabza

Einar Jónsson wasn't the first to see the ship entombed in the rocks, but little did I know then, he was one of the few Icelanders who could actually do something about it. "If I only had enough time," he said to me, as we stood on the black sand and stared at the tell-tale stones, "and sharp enough chisels, by God, I think I could really bring out the shape of it."

Einar pointed out over the water. It was that time of year when the air was mild and the sun wheeled round the mercurial sky, barely dipping below the horizon before arcing up again into another dawn. To the south, Iceland's ocean was a dirty mirror, its tarnish glittering with every churn of the breakers. "Look, Gunnar," Einar said. "Have you really looked at it? It seems like it doesn't need much work."

"It's a fisherman's yarn," I said.

"It's three great sails," said Einar.

"It's *reynisdrangar*. A beautiful cluster of rocks in the sea, all in a row, that just happen to be shaped like great sails."

"It's a troll ship."

"Einar." I kicked at the coarse, black sands by my feet. "Come now."

"And I suppose you believe now that God is a fairytale, too?"

I studied my friend critically. He had been away for a long, long time. First studying sculpture in Rome, then living and working in Copenhagen. We had exchanged letters, now and again, but letters move slowly and anyway, they are not the same. Not when as boys, we could run across the green, green fields of Galtafell, where the sheep are fat and the days sweet and slow, and be napping in the cozy bunks of each other's *baðstofa* well before noon. Back then, we'd been closer than natural brothers, able to predict what the other was thinking before he himself knew. But now? "Of course not," I said. "But Einar, we're not boys anymore. You and I both know that no great, ancient troll ship ever tried to storm the beaches at Dyrhólaey, and froze into stone when the dawn fog suddenly lifted and revealed the sun. Those are just rocks."

Einar frowned. His frown was still the same, dark as an autumnal storm. "Trolls," he said, firmly.

I sighed. "Forget the trolls. Look, the sun's peeped out. Let's go wading before it disappears."

Einar appeared to drop it. We waded and ate the lunch we'd packed, tender *hangikjöt* on rye bread, but all through the morning Einar kept giving morbid looks full of meaning to those craggy stones. As the tide receded, more of the "troll ship" appeared, the wet coloring the rough basalt. You could just see where the "sails" connected to the "deck." It really was a lovely formation, and the whole point of our journey together was to see more of the southern coast, but I didn't want to look at it too much. It would only encourage him.

"I suppose it's only a wild fancy," said Einar at last, when we finally trudged up the beach.

The fishing hamlet of Vík í Mýrdal awaited us, hunkered down in the dusty black dunes. Like much of the area, or indeed much of Iceland altogether, the modern age had not yet arrived there, though of course I only knew this because Einar had told me. I'd never had a reason to go so far as Europe.

"Well," I said. "Don't worry about the fancy. I heard somewhere that you have a creative mind. Forget it."

"I will. After we go out and take a look."

"After we *what*?"

"Take a look," Einar repeated, solemnly. "We'll ask around the village. Find a fisherman to take us out to the rocks tomorrow, in exchange for a day's labor."

"You're mad. We won't be able to get that close. The rocks below the waterline will snap us to pieces."

"What do you know of it? You're a farmer."

"So are you."

"We'll be fine."

"I'm not going."

"You'd leave me to die alone? At sea?"

"I am *not going*, Einar. And neither are you."

But back in the hamlet, Einar charmed the first fisherman's wife he met into offering us a place in their *baðstofa* for the evening, and later, her husband into giving us a place in his boat upon the morrow.

So we went. Damn it all.

*

Einar, I suppose, had seen something of the sea, having traveled across it twice. I've never been further away from Iceland than Heimaey, and even that short trip was unpleasant enough. I didn't get seasick, but the boat did become beset by a flock of kittiwakes ("Welcome to Heimaey, sir; is that bird shit in your hair?") so excuse me if I don't trust boats or the men who steer them.

The fisherman who rowed us out was named Olaf Sigurðsson, a red-faced barrel of a man with oilskin clothes that stank and a gap-toothed grin that wouldn't quit. He sang to himself in a creaky tenor as he manned one pair of oars while Einar and I gamely took turns with the other. The bastard got a lot of work out of us since he insisted on leaving at dawn, and dawn near the summer solstice happens at around, oh, 3 a.m. "Tired yet, boys?" he finally cackled, as he hauled up the anchor for the last time. "Sitting on your rears and watching sheep all day isn't quite like hauling up fish in this sun, now, is it?"

Einar smiled. A loose fish flopped about his ankles, its lips popping breathlessly. "It certainly isn't. How long have you been at this work now?"

"Oh, about 40, 45 years," said Olaf. He jerked his grizzled chin at the nearby *reynisdrangar*, to indicate that we should bring the boat round. Olaf rested his oars on the gunwales as I pulled. "Been out to the troll ship dozens of times, it's perfectly safe if you just know where to anchor and when. The kids love to see it, you know. Soon as we get near, they scream and carry on like I don't know what-all. Whoops." Olaf looked up. The temperamental coastal weather was turning, and a thick flock of clouds, gray and low, scudded into the harbor and swallowed the sun. "Well, about time. Could use a good cooling off. Whoa, Gunnar my friend, close enough!"

I stopped pulling and Olaf dropped the anchor. We were near the rocks that were furthest from the shore, close enough to see fulmars wheeling up and down the irregular cliff-face in alarm at our proximity. On either side of us, the receding tide made powerful eddies above unseen hazards, but our little vessel just quivered in its place.

"Now you know the story of the troll ship, of course, don't you?" Olaf asked.

"Oh yes," said Einar.

"It was a year and a day after the beginning of the world ..." began Olaf, as though Einar hadn't spoken.

I tuned them out. Let the two fools be dazzled by each other. Instead, I peered more closely at the basalt rock face, studying the birds wheeling through the thickening mist.

That is, until it moved.

I blinked. There were so many fulmars, I was seeing things.

No I wasn't. The rock face did it again. The movement was barely detectable, a glacial undulation of stone, as though the rock were the hide of a monster inhaling.

Or a sail, filling.

I couldn't speak. I could only swallow and point. My other hand flapped madly at Einar's shoulder.

"For pity's sake, Gunnar, what is it?"

The fog abruptly thinned. A blot of white appeared behind the clouds, growing brighter as the wind pushed them away. The rock face stilled. "It was ... I saw ..."

"Trolls," said Olaf good-naturedly, and laughed. "Usually only the littlest kids say they can spot 'em, but you must have a good eye!"

Einar laughed with him. I sagged on my seat and couldn't even manage a smile.

"Well, if that'll be all?" asked Olaf.

"It will," said Einar. "I'm so happy I could see it up close. Thank you very much, Olaf. This day has been most instructive."

*

After we came ashore, as we three settled in for a nap, Einar whispered to me, "You saw it too, didn't you, Gunnar?"

I opened my eyes. We were napping in Olaf's *baðstofa* while his wife minded the children outside. In the dim light, filtered through fishskin-covered windows, Olaf snored in his small bunk. On the floor in front of me knelt Einar, his grave eyes searching my face.

For the first time since this visit had begun, I felt that I could read his thoughts, like the old days. "Yes," I whispered back. "I saw it."

"I have to carve it."

"You're mad, Einar."

"Think of it. If I can somehow cut away all that excess stone, smooth it out, bring out the shape of the sails... I mean not literally I alone, it's far too big—but a team of us, somehow, for it will take many men ... I know a man in Copenhagen, no, two civil engineers who know how to take raw rock and—"

"Stop it."

"The sails, Gunnar. Think of it. We take all the dross away, the crags and the bird shit, and we shape the features just a bit, just a little bit. From the shore, on the nights when the moon is high, you'd be able to see that whole beautiful, terrible ship, forever frozen in the sea, and its three sails billowing."

"It would set the entombed monsters free!"

Olaf's snoring paused. I cringed. Einar's eyes bore into mine, our mutual agitation frozen until the fisherman's breath began again to putter. "I wouldn't," Einar whispered. "They're trapped. You can't ever completely free a troll once it's turned to stone. Everyone knows that."

"But nobody's ever tried what you're proposing."

"Nobody's ever been positioned to. But I am. Iceland has a magic humming deep in its bones, Gunnar, and the entire reason I went away was to learn exactly how to reveal it to ourselves, so that we can never forget."

"And you *can* reveal it! But you can do it by making some nice, normal, little statues in that new studio of yours out in Reykjavík when you return home!"

Einar's autumnal frown came on. He shook his head. His eyes were distant, glittering, like the mirrored surface of the ocean churning over its secrets. "We need to begin with a test," he said. "Yes. A little test carving, to see how workable the stone actually is. I didn't study much stone-cutting, you know, but I know a few things. I've got one small chisel with me. And I'm sure Olaf has a mallet I can borrow."

I sat up. "We are not doing this."

"'Give your eldest son another day off from fishing,' I'll say to Olaf. 'It's no trouble at all.'"

"I said—"

Again Olaf's snoring paused. I reigned in my tone to a soft and desperate hiss. "I mean it this time, Einar. *We are not doing this.*"

Einar eyed me. He rose from his kneeling position on the floor and strolled to the bunk Olaf had given him. "You're right," he said, coolly. "*We* are not. I am, alone. I don't think having you along tomorrow will be very constructive, after all."

"Einar!"

"I know you, Gunnar. You'll try to stop me. Don't pretend that you won't."

I couldn't lie to him—truly couldn't. All I could do was hiss his name in frustration. "Einar!"

The sculptor lay down and pulled his blanket up to his chin. In his mind, the matter was clearly settled.

Well, fine. If he wouldn't let me come with him, I'd have to stop him another way. I'd just find another fisherman who'd agree to take me out in his own boat and give chase.

*

The next day dawned chill and rainy. I pretended to sleep as Einar and Olaf dressed and slipped from the *baðstofa*, then sprinted like a fox to the house of Björn and Ingi Ísólfsson, twin brothers who seemed to move more slowly than the undulating *reynis-drangar* themselves. It was all I could do to stand still while they calmly readied their boat, dropping in new rope in careful, fat coils inch by excruciatingly gradual inch.

We finally made it out to sea. The wind was restless, and the water, choppy. I didn't like the look of the sky, but when I asked Björn and Ingi, "Storm coming on?" all I received was a laconic, "Maybe."

The wind rose. A heavy fog whipped in, covering the bay in fleecy dimness. We fished in silence. The catch was poor. The waves grew rougher, and several times, under Ingi's direction, we had to stop and move from one part of the boat to another to steady it. "Should we go in?" I asked, nervously.

"Maybe," said Ingi.

I started to argue my case, but the wind carried a cheery creaking to my ears—Olaf singing somewhere in the fog. If Einar wasn't quitting, neither was I. "Actually. Can we go now? To the *reynisdrangar*?"

The twins looked at each other. The sound of Olaf's boat receded.

"I have a feeling," I said. "Please. Listen, you're barely catching anything as it is. Take me now and I'll come out in the boat with you tomorrow, too. Please?"

The twins looked at each other again. God in Heaven, how is it possible for two men to turn their heads so slowly?

"Maybe," said Ingi.

My bargaining turned to begging, and my begging turned frantic and unmanly. Ingi finally relented with a sharp and uncomfortable, "Fine." I had embarrassed him. I was embarrassed myself, and we rowed to the rocks with me hanging my head in red-faced shame.

When we reached the basalt, my shame was joined by fear. Olaf's craft was moored right up against a rock face, wriggling frantically in the waves while a handful of accompanying children on board squealed and screamed in delight. No sign of Einar. My fear grew like the rising winds. "Bring me close."

"This is as close as we get," said Ingi, bringing up the oars. He wouldn't look at me.

"I need to get to the rock face!"

"Olaf's in the only good spot," said Björn. "No other place to risk landing."

I stood. "Must I throw myself overboard and swim there?"

"If you want to," said Ingi, "that's your business."

I squeezed my hands into panicked fists, nearly ready to charge into Ingi and knock him overboard myself. I looked up at the cliff face, receding upward into darkness and fog, and when the wind shifted, I caught the unmistakable sound of steel chipping into stone. *Ching, ching, ching.* "He's up there, doing it already!" I cried. "Can't you hear it? Don't you know what that madman is trying to do?"

"Time to go back," said Ingi to Björn. "We're done for the day."

"Please!" I shouted. In Olaf's boat, the children reached out tiny hands, daring to just touch the basalt before pulling away with a joyful shriek. The rock was more alive than ever, breathing and settling, breathing and settling, a ghoulish backdrop to Olaf's laughter and the high peals of Einar's madness. *Ching, ching, ching.* "Please—he's trying to carve the stone! Don't you know what that would do? It would free the ..." I was suddenly aware of how foolish I sounded. My ravings sputtered out. "... the troll ship ..."

The twins looked at each other.

Then Ingi turned his head to Olaf. "Olaf," he called. "Move your boat."

My thanks gushed forth. The twins seemed not to hear. Olaf and Ingi called out to each other, and masterful Olaf finally maneuvered his craft away from the cleft he'd wedged it into—choppy seas, swirling tides, screaming children, and all.

Ingi and Björn worked to take his place. Their boat lodged with a jolt. Where we were moored, there was no shelf or landing. Only dark, weather-beaten cliff face, towering over the pounding waves. "Up you go," said Ingi, nodding. "There's plenty of hand-holds. Don't look down."

I didn't.

Spray licked my calves and soaked my legs, despite the foul oil-skin clothes Björn had loaned me. Wet wind blinded me. The handholds were slick but sharp, like crumbled glass, and as I climbed, I cut my palms and yowled as sea salt rubbed into the wounds. A fulmar screamed past my ear, a flash of angry white that nearly made me lose my grip as I moved too near its perch. It wheeled round and dove at me. I leaned away and my foothold crumpled.

My toes kicked out for a grip and hit nothing but void. I cried out and clung on with nerveless fingers, begging Our Lord and Savior to see me through this.

A strong hand closed down upon mine. A merciful angel pulled me upward, to a hidden ledge in the lee of the wind. But God has a strange sense of humor, and this angel came in the guise of a terrible fool indeed.

"Gunnar!" said Einar, pulling me in from the edge. "You've got to be careful up here! How are you? You all right?" He looked me up and down, his grin awful and out of a place on a man who had almost watched his friend die. "I'm so glad you came after all! You've got to see this—*someone* has got to see this. The basalt, it's so weathered, it just crumbles right away. And the ship—sweet Lord bless me, it's right there waiting underneath. Look, Gunnar! Look at what marvels the chisel can free!"

I looked.

I know now what it means to be sick with terror. It means vertigo and roaring in your ears, and spots of blackness in front of your eyes, and a terminal weakness in your knees. Einar caught me in a near-swoon. "Isn't it magnificent?" he cried.

It was not. It was monstrous. A single arm, grotesque and gargantuan, writhed oh so slowly on the surface of that breathing, heaving stone. In my faint delirium, I could imagine the outline of the rest of the beast, a rude suggestion of a creature lying supine in the arch of a gigantic window or doorway. The massive arm, so much crisper now that Einar had worked it over, dangled down to the ledge we stood upon. Its great, hooked claws undulated within inches of Einar's abandoned chisel and mallet.

The wind shifted. My back was hit with a wall of icy wet, and another wave of vertigo overtook me. I dropped to my knees. Einar raved on, squinting into the wind and shouting into the roar, one finger pointing and waving behind him. "Isn't it a wonder? Those claws, those knucklebones, those sinews and joints. You can nearly see it flexing!"

Nearly? I did. The arm flexed. With a terrible, grinding boom, those claws tore free of the stone and reached down.

"Just think of what the *Alþingi* will say when I tell them of this! Just think of the glory we can reveal, right here in the shadow of Dyrhólaey, moored off the coast for all ages and all time!"

The claws grasped Einar's sharpened chisel.

"Greater than the Pyramids! The Colossus at Rhodes! Or even China's Great Wall!"

I screamed.

Einar turned. The arm lashed out. I threw myself forward, wrapping my own arms around Einar's shock-frozen body, my face mashing into his soaked and filthy oilskin. We skidded along the ledge, beneath the full length of the arm, but with a sound like deafening thunder, more of the limb tore free. I didn't even see the chisel coming after us. I only felt the wind of it against my neck.

Ching-ching-ching. Basalt hailed down upon us, into my hair, stinging my eyes. The thing was striking blindly, but that luck wouldn't last long. I rubbed one eye free of grit and looked up.

The chisel was raised high, ready to plunge into Einar's heart.

I kicked off the breathing wall and rolled, pulling Einar away from the deathblow. But I rolled too far. The ledge vanished beneath me, and then there was nothing but wet wind whistling in my ears and Einar's heartbeat slamming against my arms.

I didn't even have time for a prayer.

*

Luck was with us. Instead of striking rocks, we plunged into the sea, and instead of breaking anything, we only nearly drowned. The remainder of our visit together, instead of being spent gamboling innocently over the countryside, was spent recovering under the thorough but taciturn care of Björn and Ingi. Considering that we had very nearly lost our lives, I didn't mind.

I returned to Galtafell. Einar returned to his new studio in Reykjavík. As before, we sent each other letters, but also as before, it was not the same. He was very busy with work. He got married. He moved to America for a time, and became quite famous. His letters became infrequent, and eventually trickled to nothing.

I remained on the family farm and dreamed about the *reynis-*

drangar—about what writhes upon a certain hidden ledge, on days dark and foggy, a rusted chisel clutched in a misshapen fist. I dream that it knows what to do, so that it may someday free its brothers from the shadow of Dyrhólaey. *Ching, ching, ching.*

Einar's work has become strange and fantastic, now, in his old age. Angels, homunculi, giants, gods, wolves, monsters, crucifixes, Madonnas, tangled together in symmetric, mystical clumps loaded with anxiety and symbolism many people cannot understand. He's very spiritual now, they say, becoming more and more devout as time goes on, becoming enmeshed in pondering the unknowable.

But this is wrong. Even across such time and distance as lies between us now, to some degree, his thoughts are still mine, and I know from what obsession his tangled phantasms spring.

He dreams about that rusted chisel, too, and is afraid.

***

KJ Kabza's work has appeared in Nature, F&SF, Daily Science Fiction, Beneath Ceaseless Skies, Flash Fiction Online, *and others, and has been called "Delightful" (*Locus Online*), "Very clever, indeed" (*SFRevu*), "Intelligent and sublime" (*Tangent*), and "Fascinatingly weird" (*Brit Mandelo*). He has seen the troll ship (in renisdrangar form) off the Icelandic coast of Vík with his own eyes, as well as the Einar Jónsson museum in Reykjavík, and regrets to say that he cannot prove that his story in this anthology is not a total fabrication. For updates on forthcoming releases and links to free fiction, he invites you to follow him on Twitter @KJKabza and peruse www.kjkabza.com*

Oldest Friends

William Gerke

Kent McCord rolled out from under the bed to discover that the house had changed overnight.

He stood, brushed the dust from his uniform, polished his badge with this sleeve, and inspected Lizzie's room. The bed remained the same—sturdy, wooden, dark—but there were new scratches on the headboard and a pile of quilts instead of Lizzie's familiar moon-and-stars blanket. An empty suitcase sat atop the bed and someone had covered the dresser with stacks of books and magazines. A wardrobe full of sweaters and long dresses had replaced Lizzie's toy chest.

What had happened? Everything had been normal the night before. This was a mystery, but Kent was good at mysteries. He and Lizzie had solved many of them.

The hallway and living room had changed as well. The wood paneling was gone. The walls were painted white, and someone had crammed new furniture everywhere. Not new, Kent corrected himself, just new to him. The end tables, extra chair, ottoman, credenza, and the big baskets full of magazines and yarn all showed signs of wear. Only the two faded paintings above the couch remained the same.

Dusty picture frames covered every flat surface. Kent scanned them quickly. He was a police officer, trained to notice details. Many of the people shared family traits. He shifted some frames and found familiar pictures behind them. They were faded, but they were the same photos he had looked at before going to bed: the family vacation in Colorado, Lizzie's kindergarten graduation, Mr. and Mrs. Olson's wedding, Grammy and Gramps' anniversary.

Kent decided that he had better talk with Baboo.

He forced himself to remain calm as he climbed the stairs. The door to the spare room stood open. The walls were still blue, but they had faded like the paintings, and all the furniture was gone. Stacks of boxes filled the small bedroom, but the little utility door built into the wall was unblocked. Boxes were scattered around it, contents spilled out, as if someone had been searching for something. Photos, magazines, and keepsakes sat in piles on the floor.

Kent knelt beside the door and knocked.

"Baboo?" he asked. "Are you there?"

The door creaked open. A pale hand emerged, twice the size of a human hand and covered in hair.

"Yeah. What is it?"

"Something's happened to the house," said Kent. "It's changed."

"The whole house?"

"My room, the living room, your room. I haven't seen the rest."

"Well, it was bound to happen," said Baboo. "Things have changed before."

"Yes, but not like this. Not everything at once."

Sometimes a piece of furniture would appear or disappear.

Once the whole dining room changed color because Lizzie's mom painted it. But never like this.

"What do you want me to tell you, Kent? I don't know what happened or why. You're the cop. You figure it out."

The hand retreated, pulling the door closed behind it.

"And don't forget to put the kettle on," said the muffled voice. "The others will be here soon."

Kent grimaced. Baboo was being more surly than usual. He would have to solve this mystery on his own.

Back downstairs, the kitchen had changed as well. The cupboards were the same, but all the appliances were different; the refrigerator was white, and the stove had more lights and dials. The lace curtains over the sink were not the ones he remembered, but they were faded and yellow with age. A dark blue kettle sat on the stove instead of the old silver one. Kent filled it with water and lit the stove. He set the table. The china was the same, if a little more chipped and scratched. He found a package of cookies in the pantry and placed them on one of the old china plates.

The others would arrive shortly, but Kent thought he still had time to investigate. He would start looking for clues back in the bedroom.

He found his first one the moment he entered. A woman knelt beside the bed, reaching under it, searching for something.

"Can I help you, ma'am?" he said.

She turned her head at the sound of his voice and stood up slowly. She had probably never been tall, but age had bent her back. Short hair lay in soft swoops upon her head, and watery, blue eyes blinked behind thin-rimmed glasses. She held a single silver earring.

"Kent?" she said. "Thank goodness you're here. My other earring is under the bed, where I can't reach. Could you be a dear and get it?"

Kent knelt and wriggled into his little home under the bed. Something glittered beside the stack of Young Explorer magazines that he read and re-read each night. He picked it up. When he stood up, the room was empty

The suitcase on the bed was full now. He set the earring on a pile of neatly-folded sweaters. Beside it, atop a stack of slacks, was a brochure.

"Sunset Villa," he read. "Assisted living, elder care, and rehabilitation."

The brochure spoke about housing for elderly couples and individuals, care for people with dementia, Alzheimer's and other age-related conditions. It used phrases like "resident-centered care" and "nurturing environment" and "dignified, meaningful activities." The pictures showed clean, spacious rooms and happy staff in brightly-colored uniforms wheeling cheerful old people around.

Old people.

Folding the brochure and tucking it into his back pocket, Kent ran to the living room.

He went through the pictures. He grabbed the one of Lizzie's kindergarten graduation. He found one of a family standing next to a picnic table and one of a high school graduation. In a few minutes, he had assembled a line of photos. He traced the faces with a finger. They were all the same person, sliced out of time—his Lizzie, grown up and grown old.

The doorbell rang.

Kent touched the last picture gently. It was the woman from the bedroom. Her hair was a little darker, her skin a little smoother, and she wasn't wearing glasses. The man in the picture with her looked gaunt, with hollows under his eyes and sallow skin, but his smile was full of joy as he looked at Lizzie.

The doorbell rang again.

When Kent answered the door, Baku-Baku waited on the front step, holding a plate of tuna and cucumber sandwiches with his fins.

"What's up, Kent?" he asked. His breath stank of the sea. "You look like you've seen a ghost."

"It's been a strange morning," said Kent.

The shark hopped into the house on his tail and followed Kent into the dining room. He put the plate of sandwiches on the table.

"The place has changed," said Baku-Baku.

Before Kent could say anything, the doorbell rang again and the teapot whistled. Baku-Baku offered to take care of the tea while Kent answered the door.

Mortimer and Annie were both there. Annie was taller than Kent, willowy and thin. She had to be to live in the walls of her house. Mortimer seemed miniscule by comparison. His long pointed ears, curled shoes, and green tights marked him clearly as an elf. He lived in a tree but always came indoors for tea. Not all the elves in the neighborhood were that friendly.

Kent took their coats and hung them in the closet.

"Thank you for coming," he said.

"Thank you for having us," said Mortimer.

Annie kissed Kent on the cheek and looked around. "What happened?" she asked.

Baku-Baku called out that tea was ready. The trio joined him around the kitchen table. Kent hosted, filling each teacup, offering cream and lumps of sugar. When he heard a familiar scuttling on the stairs, he filled Baboo's cup. A moment later, Baboo pulled himself up the chair leg with long fingers, leaping from there to the table. The hand couldn't drink tea or eat, but that never stopped him from joining them.

"To Lizzie," said Kent. The others echoed him, clinking their cups in the traditional first toast to their absent hostess.

"Kent was just going to tell us about the changes to the house," Baku-Baku told Baboo.

"I think it happened because Lizzie is back," said Kent. "That's when things would change before."

"Don't be foolish," said Baboo. "Lizzie's been gone for seventy years. Why would she suddenly come back?"

"I don't know. But I saw a woman in the bedroom who seemed to know me." He gestured towards the row of photos in the living room. "I think it's Lizzie."

"It's probably just a new friend wandered in from outside. That happens sometimes. She'll poke around for a few days and vanish, like that cat."

"Teakettle visited a couple of times when Lizzie was young," said Ken. "But nothing changed when he showed up. This is different."

"I'll say," said Baku-Baku. "I don't think I've ever seen a house change this much since Mortimer's- er, I mean, Annie's house."

The others nodded; Mortimer looked pained. Unlike Baboo and Kent, who had arrived around the same time, Annie had appeared in the walls of Mortimer's house years after his friend,

Debbie, had vanished. She knew nothing of Debbie but spoke, instead, of a girl named Katie. The house had changed, and Mortimer had struggled to adapt, spending more and more time in his tree. Eventually, Katie had gone as well, leaving Annie behind in the walls.

"If it's Lizzie, she must have come back for a reason," said Annie. "Maybe she'll come back again."

"Don't be stupid, Annie," said Baboo.

"Baboo!" said Kent, sharply. "That was uncalled for. Annie's a guest."

"But you're both being stupid. She's an old woman. She can't be Lizzie!"

Annie gasped. Mortimer paled. Baku-Baku chewed his sandwich.

"I didn't say she was old," said Kent quietly.

"You said she was a woman," said Baboo. "That means she's old."

"The boxes were all a mess in the spare room," said Kent. "They'd been pulled away from your door. She was up there, and you saw her. That's when the house changed. And you didn't say anything!"

"Sure, I saw some old lady," said Baboo. "But that doesn't mean it's her. Lizzie left us years ago, and she's not coming back. That's how it goes. Everyone here knows it." He pointed at Baku-Baku. "You don't see him waiting around for Connor to come back. Or Mortimer pining after Debbie. It's been seventy years. Get over it!" Baboo dropped off the table and scuttled out of the dining room. A moment later, they heard the clump of his utility door slamming.

The tea party sat in silence. Mortimer sipped his tea. Annie looked at her hands. Baku-Baku sniffed.

"I do wish Connor would come back," said the shark softly. "I miss him."

Annie squeezed his fin.

"Baku-Baku's right," said Mortimer. "I miss Debbie, too. If you think Lizzie is back, you need to find her."

"She was packing a suitcase," he said, showing them the brochure. "And this was on the bed. If I'm right, and it really is Lizzie—but older—I think she may be going here."

"You should go there right away," said Mortimer. "You don't want to miss her. And if she appears here, Baboo will be around to see her."

"You're right," said Kent. "I'm sorry I'll have to cut tea time short."

"It's okay," said Annie. "It was our suggestion. We'll help you clear up."

Mortimer carried cups and plates to the sink. Kent washed, and Annie dried and put away the dishes. Baku-Baku put several of his sandwiches in an old tin he found in a cupboard. He presented them to Kent as they left.

"For your trip," said the shark. "You don't know how long you'll be gone, and you might get hungry."

"Thank you, Baku-Baku."

"Tea is at my place tomorrow," said Mortimer. "Come back if you can and tell us what you learned."

"I will," said Kent.

He shook Mortimer's hand and hugged Annie

"Can you come by later and check on Baboo?" he asked. "I'm

worried about leaving him alone. Especially after our fight."

Annie smiled. "Of course."

Kent watched them walk to their homes. They all lived in neighboring houses and didn't have far to go. He was the only one with a car.

He gathered his things—the sandwiches, the brochure, his hat, the car keys—and made sure all the doors and windows were locked. There were monsters in the neighborhood that would get in and make mischief if he wasn't careful. Things would be back to normal the next day, but it upset Baboo. He left a note telling where he had gone and reminding Baboo that tea was at Mortimer's. Then he walked to his car.

Kent kept his police cruiser parked at the entrance to the cul-de-sac to deter any criminals. That had been Lizzie's idea. The glove compartment held maps of the town, the state, most of the United States, Africa, Timbuktu, Oz, and Wonderland. He set the brochure and the map of town on the passenger seat before buckling in and starting the car.

Kent drove carefully, consulting the map often. The streets were the same, but old buildings had been torn down and new ones put up. At the edge of town, where there had been fields and woods, he found huge buildings with bright signs and vast parking lots.

Beyond them, he saw the sign for Sunset Villa. Buildings of varying heights clustered around a central courtyard like a child's blocks stacked in uneven piles. Parking lots were labeled "Staff", "Resident", and "Visitor." The visitor lot was nearly empty. Kent parked in the back.

The lobby was bright and clean. A flowery border ran along the wall, and paintings of mountains, valleys, forests, and farms hung above it—windows into a world that existed far away. Behind the broad reception desk nestled offices full of papers. They might contain useful information, but Kent decided to do some exploring first, hoping to run into Lizzie.

Kent wandered the halls for hours. The complex, he discovered, was divided into sections connected by walkways, lounges, and dining rooms. One section contained small apartments with kitchenettes and separate bedrooms. Another housed individual bedrooms. Another had shared rooms. The shared rooms, with their dividing curtains, reminded Kent of the nursing home where they had visited Grammy Olson. That was after Gramps had died, and she hadn't been able to take care of herself.

Pictures hung beside the rooms, names printed beneath them: Roger Wells, Angela Sawyer, Carter Burke. Some smiled and some frowned. Others looked confused and sad. All of them were old.

One bore Lizzie's name. The picture was of the woman from her bedroom.

It was one of the single rooms. The curtains were pulled back, and sunlight warmed the room. She had a good view of the visitors' lot, and Kent could see his car. The rest of the room felt sterile: a neatly-made single bed, a low dresser with six drawers, a chair by the window, an empty bulletin board. A door led to a tiny but functional bathroom.

Kent decided he would wait. Lizzie had been packing in the morning. She might not have moved in yet.

He took off his coat and settled in the chair. When the cool, blue glow of the parking lot lights replaced the warmth of the sun, he crawled under the bed. It felt unfamiliar and cold. He made a pillow of his coat, and eventually, he slept.

The next day, Kent waited some more. He grew bored. He didn't want to miss Lizzie when she arrived, but he also wanted to know more. He decided to check the offices for clues.

From behind the reception desk, he heard the whistling of a kettle. He followed the noise deeper into the twisty little maze of hallways to a room marked "Kitchen."

The kitchen was a small room with a pair of tables, a refrigerator, a line of bright yellow cabinets, and a two-burner stove. A boy stood on a plastic chair beside the stove. He looked five or six years old. Wavy, sandy hair hung over his ears, and he wore blue jeans, sneakers, and a paisley shirt. When he saw Kent, his freckled face split in a big smile.

"Hello!" he said. "I'm David."

He pronounced the two syllables distinctly: "Day-vid."

"Hello, David," said Kent. "My name is Kent McCord."

"Like in the TV show?" asked David.

"Yes. Like in the TV show."

Lizzie's father had watched One Adam-12. Sometimes Lizzie got to stay up late and watch it with him. She would tell Kent about his fictional namesake's adventures.

David offered tea, and Kent volunteered to pour. The boy fished another tea bag out of a drawer and got a second mug from the cupboard.

"It'll be nice to have someone here again," said David. "The last company I had was a talking dog named Ulf. Before that, there was a cowboy who called himself Cowboy and a robot named Charlie. Cowboy was all right, but Charlie would just sit and beep and didn't drink tea or like to play games."

"What were they doing here?"

"Visiting their friends. That's why you're here, isn't it? You've got a friend and he's here now."

"She's here," said Kent. "At least, I've seen her picture."

"Well, if you've seen her picture and you're here, then she's here. It's just like back in your house, right? She's there, but she's not always around. If you stay here, though, you'll see her eventually."

Kent set the mugs on the table. David dragged his chair over and climbed into it. They participated in the oldest ritual—milk or sugar, one lump or two.

"You seem to know an awful lot," said Kent.

"I've been around. I'm almost eighty, and I've been here for five years. You start to figure things out."

"Like what?"

"Like how your friend looks older and we don't. You see—" He stopped and cocked his head. "Sorry, Kent. I've gotta go."

David rushed out the door, his sneakers slapping on the linoleum floors. Ken followed, adult legs keeping up with the boy.

"Is everything okay?" asked Kent.

"It's fine. Arthur's back, so I've gotta get to him."

"How do you know?"

"I just know. Like he's a humming in the back of my head, you know?"

"I've never felt that."

"You will. It's different at home. They're just there, and you're there. This place is bigger, so when they appear you've gotta go to them. But you'll feel it. Cowboy did."

David picked up speed as they went, nearly running through

the halls. Kent stretched his legs to keep up. They passed through a common space and down a wide hallway that Kent recognized as the same hallway Lizzie's room was on. Residents shuffled down the hall or sat in wheelchairs against the wall. Blue-scrubbed staff navigated around them or helped them to their destinations. Two people argued on the television in a nearby common room.

David darted inside one of the rooms, avoiding the resident standing in the doorway, but Kent found that he couldn't follow the boy. The resident in the doorway was Lizzie.

Kent couldn't believe that he hadn't recognized her right away. The blue eyes, the soft cheeks, the slightly rounded nose, all belonged to little Lizzie.

"Hello, Kent," she said.

"Hello, Lizzie."

"I'm glad you're here. I was starting to think I was all alone."

She was reaching out to give him a hug, when a man in a white doctor's coat bumped them, knocking them apart. The doctor glared at Lizzie.

"Someone get her out of here," he shouted over his shoulder. "Clear this hallway."

The doctor joined a pair of blue-scrubbed orderlies around a bed. The man in the bed twisted and writhed, his back arching. Lizzie pressed up against the door-frame, watching. Her eyes were wide.

"Something's wrong with him," she said, indicating the man in the bed.

"I think he might be sick."

"The doctor will help him then. Although he's very angry for a doctor."

Kent agreed. The man had not seemed pleasant. A woman approached them, filling the hallway in her blue scrubs. Her frown did not match the laugh lines around her eyes. She took Lizzie by the arm and tugged her away from the door.

"Lizzie, hon, what are you doing?"

"I heard people shouting. Kent and I wanted to see what's was going on."

The woman looked around, frowned again, and then smiled. Her face opened up with that smile.

"Oh, Kent. Your daughter said you were talking about him on the drive over. Why don't you just wait inside your room, and Kent will find out what's going on."

"That sounds like a good idea," said Lizzie. "Come down in a couple of minutes. I'll have tea for you, and we can talk."

"I'll do that," said the big nurse, gently guiding Lizzie toward her chair. "I like a nice cup of tea."

"I wasn't talking to you." Lizzie looked back over her shoulder at Kent. "I wasn't talking to her."

"I know," he said. "I'll be there in a minute."

The nurse pulled Lizzie away, fussing over her. Inside the room, David was shouting. His voice quavered with fear and rage. With Lizzie gone, the doctor and orderlies faded away. Kent could only see David, standing at the foot of the bed, waving his arms and shouting.

"Stop it! Get away from him! It hurts. It's not helping, and all it does is hurt." David looked at Kent. Tears washed his cheeks. "They're hurting him. And there's nothing I can do."

Kent looked down at his hands. He couldn't see the people that

David saw. They were part of Arthur's world, not Lizzie's. He had learned how that worked from Mortimer and Annie.

"I'm sorry," he said and did the only thing he could.

Kent took the boy in his arms and held him close. David buried his face in Kent's uniform and sobbed, murmuring angry, fearful words. Kent rubbed his back and fought back sympathetic tears. After a moment, David stiffened. He looked up at Kent. Tear tracks streaked his cheeks, but he had stopped crying.

"Oh, that's how it works," he said softly. He smiled. "Thanks for being here with me at the end. I'm glad that I wasn't alone, but I have to go now."

Tears filled Kent's eyes, blurring his vision. He felt the boy go limp and slack in his arms, and when he blinked away the tears, David was gone.

Kent looked around, wiping his eyes. The room was identical to Lizzie's except that a small television sat on top of the dresser and the bulletin board was covered in pictures. Someone had closed the curtains, leaving everything shrouded and dim. A single line of golden light from the narrow space between them drew a sharp line across the bed. The sheets had been pulled all the way up, covering a lumpish form.

Kent pulled them back. An old man lay beneath. His pajama top was closed, but no one had taken the time to button it. Pale flesh and gray hair were visible in the gaps. He wasn't breathing.

Arthur was dead.

Kent covered the body with the sheet.

This was another mystery, like when the house had changed. He needed to put together all the pieces of the puzzle, and it would make sense. When Arthur was alive, he was invisible. Now that he was dead, Kent could see him, and David had vanished. Normally, Kent could only see other people when Lizzie was around. When she was gone, he remained behind, and the world stayed the same. The only people in it were people like him or Mortimer or David—people with friends like Lizzie. People who didn't disappear.

Kent frowned. He had never had to think about how the world worked before. When he was younger, he had just laughed and played with Lizzie, enjoying her company and passing time with Baboo when she wasn't there. During the long time without her, he'd lived a simple life with Baboo in the unchanging house. Lizzie's reappearance had complicated everything.

David had seemed to understand how things worked. Kent wished the boy was still around to tell him, but he would have to figure this out on his own.

Kent remembered when Lizzie's Grammy died. She had been very old and lived in a home like Sunset Villa. When they visited, she hadn't remembered Lizzie. When Mrs. Olson told them that Grammy had gone to Heaven, Lizzie had been around quite a bit. One time, they climbed a tree to get closer to Grammy. Lizzie's mother hadn't been happy about that, and they'd spent the next few days stuck indoors playing with Baboo. Sometimes they would pretend that Grammy was having tea with them, but she hadn't really been there. She was gone forever, Mrs. Olson had explained, and Lizzie wouldn't see her again until she died and went to Heaven too.

But Arthur was there, and David was gone. He wouldn't get to see Arthur anymore. Had Mrs. Olson lied? When Lizzie died, would Kent vanish as well and never see her or Baboo again? Or when David vanished, had he gone to Heaven? Was he there with Lizzie's Grammy? Was some part of Arthur there, too, leaving behind only his body, just another object like a piece of furniture or a toy?

Kent leaned his head against the cool plaster of the wall, trembling. His mind was running in circles. He needed to see Lizzie. She always knew the answers to his questions. She would be able to help him. He stumbled down the hall.

Lizzie's room had changed. There were flowers on the dresser now, and a few pictures on the bulletin board. A framed painting of a flower hung on the wall. A rocking chair sat by the window, and one of the heavy quilts from Lizzie's bedroom covered the bed. Lizzie sat on the bed in a patch of sunlight, knitting. A bag of yarn sat beside her, its contents spilling onto the quilt. She smiled.

"Hello, Kent. How is the man down the hall?"

Kent sat down next to her. "He's gone. I think the doctors were trying to help him, but they couldn't."

"I didn't really know him."

"I didn't either, but I knew his friend, David."

"Maybe David can play with us now?"

"I don't think so."

There was a knock on the door-frame. The big nurse entered with a steaming paper cup.

"I brought your tea, hon, with milk and sugar."

"Just one cup?" asked Lizzie. "What about Kent?"

The nurse looked confused for a moment, then nodded.

"I forgot about Kent," she said. "I'll bring you an extra cup next time."

She set the tea on the bedside table and patted Lizzie's shoulder. Kent watched the nurse leave in silence, while Lizzie sipped her tea.

He wasn't sure if he appreciated the kindness or was angered by the condescension. She had acted as if she was humoring Lizzie, as if something was wrong with her. The staff here seemed to want to help the residents, but they also didn't seem to know them at all. Not like Kent and David knew their friends.

"Would you like some of my tea?" asked Lizzie.

"No thank you. I'll have some next time."

"Maybe mom and dad will visit."

Kent remembered the pictures back at the house. He looked at Lizzie, old and bent but still beautiful. He suddenly understood the nurse's actions. There was something wrong with Lizzie. She was at Sunset Villa because she could no longer take care of herself. She would not be able to solve Kent's problems, to answer his questions about the world. Age and time had brought her back to him, just as it had brought Arthur back to David. And just as surely, they would take her away. Forever.

A low sob bubbled up inside him. He tried to cover it up, but Lizzie knew him too well. She rubbed his back gently, as her mother had rubbed hers when she was scared or sick.

"Are you okay?"

"I'm fine," he said. Better than he had been for seventy years. "You're right. Maybe your mom and dad will join us next time. Maybe I could go and get Baboo."

Lizzie bounced a bit on the bed and giggled.

"Yes, Baboo. You should bring him here. He could live in the dresser."

Kent was about to agree, when Lizzie turned away, her eyes going to the door. Kent followed her gaze, but he saw nothing. When he looked back, she was gone. He couldn't feel her hand on his back. Her tea sat cooling on the table, her knitting piled beside him.

He sighed. That was how it had been in the old days. One moment she was there, the next she was gone. That was how it would be again.

Kent stood and straightened his uniform. He would go home right away. It might still be early enough to catch the others at Mortimer's tree house. He wasn't sure what he would tell them, but he had to convince Baboo to come back with him to Sunset Villa. Lizzie always liked having Baboo around. His grumpiness made her laugh, which made Baboo laugh in spite of himself.

Whether they had five years left or only a few weeks, Kent would spend them hearing the laughter of his oldest friends.

***

William Gerke *lives, works, and writes in Boston with his patient wife and their amazing son. His short fiction has been published in* Space & Time Magazine, Heroic Fantasy Quarterly, *and* Crossed Genres. *You can learn more about him and keep up with news at williamgerke.com.*

Love and the Giant Squid

Julia Rios

Her name was Healuwo, and she was lonely. Well into her brood-ing phase now, she knew she ought to be looking for a mate to fer-tilize her eggs, but instead she hovered at the edges of the north-ern landmasses, hoping for a different sort of male to appear. She'd been fascinated by humans ever since she'd first heard about them as a broodling—fantastical creatures who lived out of water, covering the landmasses with strange buildings and art. They couldn't just live in the above as it was. They had to change it. Healuwo wanted desperately to spend time with them.

Legends floated through the underwater about humans who came to reign below for decades at a time. Other squid scoffed, but Healuwo believed deep inside her soul that the stories were true, regardless of the many complications they presented. Squid couldn't breathe above water any more than humans could breathe below, and that was only the tip of the iceberg. Not that Healuwo had anything against icebergs. Sometimes they killed whales, after all.

*

I was shopping for fruit to bring to my brother's wedding picnic when I saw my father. He stood in the produce section of the grocery store in St. John's, eating grapes like it was the most normal thing in the world. I did a double take, thinking of course it couldn't be him. This guy was too young, and also my father had been dead for eight years. But then he looked right at me and said, "Honey Baloney?" And I couldn't pretend it wasn't him after he used my stupid childhood nickname. If there was anyone who'd bend the laws of nature just to spite me, it was my father.

When I say he was young, I don't mean he was a strapping lad of 20 or anything, but he wasn't as pale and shriveled as he'd been when he'd died at the age of 68. He looked vigorous. His skin was a warm, healthy brown, and his hair was truly black, unlike all the times he'd tried to dye over the grey and wound up with purple or green tints.

My father extended a hand, proffering three grapes that I might choose from. "Want one?"

I flinched, swamped with uncomfortable memories of grocery stores past. I didn't want to touch him. That would make it all too real. If I kept my distance, I could hang onto the idea that it was a hallucination, brought on by my anxiety about meeting my brother's new family. I stepped back, wary. "No. And you should pay for those."

"Still concerned with that, eh?" My father chuckled, his baritone as resonant as always, and his accent no less pronounced.

"Trina, they want me to eat them! They're samples!"

I glanced down at the half eaten bunch in front of him and decided not to argue. No one ever won arguments with my father.

"You're dead," I said, as if the affirmation would make things better. "Consuela found you in the hallway. We had you cremated."

He shrugged. "I came back. Business."

"I didn't think Newfoundland was a drug trafficking hotspot," I said.

My father popped another grape into his mouth, completely unperturbed. "It's not. I'm done with all that now."

"Then what are you doing here?"

"Something else. You know what, though?" He held a grape up to my face for inspection, and I avoided looking at it, staring instead at the scar on his index finger from when he'd cut himself while slicing an orange. I concentrated on the strange balloon shape of the tip, and on the smooth bit where his skin had grown back without a fingerprint.

"What?" I asked.

He looked around, and leaned his head in conspiratorially, overwhelming me with his all too familiar scent. Soap and sweat blended in a way that reminded me of a bitter herb, like sage that's gone off or something. I'd always hated it as a kid. I didn't know what soap he used, but if I ever found it, I'd ban it from my household so I could be sure never to smell it again.

"In Colombia they have better fruit. I miss tamarinds. You don't find tamarinds in Newfoundland."

I took another step backward, out of his circle of intimate stench. "Are you going to tell me why you're here?"

"I need an excuse to see my children? This is a family reunion, isn't it?"

My father, the same man who had abandoned Este and me when we were kids, the one who had left us with the housekeeper while he went off on drug trade adventures—this man was coming back from the dead to see us? Anger boiled up inside my chest. I wanted to say so many things to him, to hurt him like he'd hurt me, but instead, all that came out was, "You better not ruin my trip."

Jared came around the end of the cereal aisle, calling my name. I turned to look, just for a second, and when I turned back, my father was gone.

"Did you see him?" I asked, staring at the empty space by the grape display.

"Who?"

I sighed. "Never mind."

Jared stroked his one carefully cultivated tuft of chin hair and frowned. "Trina, are you all right?"

The only evidence that this hadn't been a bizarre daydream was a bunch of grapes, three quarters bare. That wasn't going to convince a skeptic like Jared.

"I'm sorry," I said, leaning in for a kiss. Jared's aftershave smelled fresh and spicy. He was nothing like my father. "I think I'm just tired. Did you find everything?"

"Crackers and cheese, check." Jared gave me a mock salute. "Did you want grapes?"

"No," I said, too quickly. "Let's just go."

*

Healuwo understood craggy shores and cold waters. She'd traveled all the northern coasts from Iceland and Greenland to Norway, Finland, Denmark, and Sweden, but she kept coming back to this place. Labrador was desolate and strange, so, inevitably she drifted south to be near the island. It had more people, and more of Healuwo's beloved English. The language of the sea was not so compartmentalized as human speech. People didn't speak as such—humans would call it telepathy. Healuwo would love to use sea language with humans, but they never seemed willing to believe in it. To make matters worse, a constant trickle of admonishment flowed across the currents each time she tried. Other squid overheard, and they all beamed back the same thing: shouldn't Healuwo be concentrating on something else?

Her broodmates had all reproduced already, each one reporting with satisfied relief, and passing judgment on Healuwo's continued non-maternal status. As the oldest, she should have been the first. The thing was, she knew if she let nature take its course, her life would no longer be hers. What little chance she had of getting close to humans, of talking to them, and sharing in their strangeness, would be gone forever.

Healuwo collected comforting things to cling to in the case of that eventuality. The best was a waterproof tablet she'd found on a diver. There had, unfortunately, been a few divers. She never meant for it to happen, but the passage of time wore on her nerves, and panic was panic.

The tablet had several e-books stored on it, and Healuwo read again and again about Captain Ahab, taking the tiny device into dark crevices, away from prying eyes. The parts about whaling fascinated her most of all. She pored over them, rubbing three arms against her mantle and wondering if perhaps someday she might find a whaler friend of her own. He'd be someone who would find her beautiful instead of monstrous, someone who would lovingly kill her predators and use their blubber for lamps, their bones for corsets, their meat for a Valentine's Day feast.

When her youngest broodmate successfully completed her brooding phase, Healuwo decided she could not wait any longer. It was now or never, she thought as she prepared to head land-wards. She was about to start climbing when a flash of red in the distance stopped her. Just her luck that she'd run into Shaluraya today of all days.

Shaluraya was next oldest of Healuwo's broodmates, and she had very conservative ideas about what it meant to be a squid.

She raised two arms in greeting as she approached Healuwo, but the tone of her gesture was more accusatory than amicable. *What are you doing?* she asked.

Healuwo hesitated. Shaluraya would not approve of her plan, and she didn't relish the thought of arguing. Everyone would find out soon enough anyway, though. Plus, Shaluraya was younger and had no authority over Healuwo, even if she did have her own brood now.

Healuwo adopted a dominant pose, spreading her lower half out as much as she could, and fanning water currents Shaluraya's way.

I'm going to the surface.

Healuwo, that's not proper. Shaluraya's arms flailed in exaggerated shock and disapproval.

Healuwo rippled her arms and her mantle, shrugging. *If you have a better way of getting humans down here, I'd love to know it.*

Shaluraya's posture grew more agitated, but Healuwo didn't stick around to hear what other criticisms she might have. Instead she sped upward with a great push. She hoped Shaluraya stumbled in the wake.

*

Esteban and I grew up too fast after our mother died, even with Consuela to look after us. She was gentle and kind, but as our housekeeper, she wasn't blood, and she didn't have any money of her own. We couldn't depend on her always being there, and all three of us knew it. No one ever knew when my father would return from his "business" trips, and we weren't sure whether to hope for or fear his surprise appearances. He was high most of the time, benevolent half of the time, and dangerous all of the time— once he came home waving a loaded gun and carelessly shot three holes in the entryway wall by way of greeting.

As long as he was still alive, we had a place to stay, though. We worried about what might become of us if he didn't come home, didn't pay the bills. I always told Este it would be okay, but even though I made tons of survival plans, I dreaded the idea of having to use them. We were lucky that the worst case scenario didn't happen until we were both adults. When our father was declared legally dead, we didn't get a wicked guardian like fairy tale children. We just got the house, and a truckload of debt, which we ended up selling the house to pay.

We turned out okay, though. I had Jared, who was sweet under the smart-mouthed surface, and Esteban found a whole family who adored him.

Kimberly had two kids from a previous marriage, and Esteban

got along with them amazingly well. He was a dream step-dad—supportive, engaged, and gentle: the exact opposite of our father. Almost every picture Este posted online showed Annie and Shane climbing all over him like he was a jungle gym. I'd met them once when they'd come down to Tampa, but it was only for one day before they headed off to Disney World. Still, they'd treated me like I was one of them. Like I belonged.

Because of the kids, and because it was a second marriage, Kimberly and Esteban decided to forgo a traditional wedding and honeymoon in favor of hosting a family reunion in Kimberly's hometown. It was the sort of bonding thing that I had craved my entire life. I should have been ecstatic, not preoccupied, but once again my father had found a way to ruin things for me.

My mind kept drifting back to my father during the short ceremony in Bowring Park, and I hardly ate when the post-ceremony picnic began, even though there was tons of delicious homemade food. While everyone else played Frisbee on the lawn outside the bungalow, I sat inside, brooding.

We went on a whale-watching cruise the next day, and I kept thinking I saw my father in the gift shop. On day three, at the top of Signal Hill, I didn't even notice the stunning views of St. John's because I was too busy examining the crowd of tourists, looking for *him*.

Este joined me by one of the cannons, away from everyone else in our group. "Trina, What's with you? I thought you really liked Kimberly and the kids. You said you were excited, before, but now it's like you don't even want to be here."

"I do," I said. "I'm sorry. I think I'm just jet-lagged or something." When Este walked away, I kicked the old stone wall, wishing it was my father.

That night we went on a ghost tour. As soon as our group arrived, the guide banged his staff on the sidewalk, activating green and purple flashing lights.

Jared snickered, and I elbowed him in the ribs.

"Don't make fun."

"Oh come on, Trina. I count on you to mock stuff with me. It's what makes us so good together."

"Doof," I said. "The kids are really excited about this. That's all I meant."

An hour later we'd walked maybe a quarter mile, and heard about several buildings with cold basements along with a few bonus stories that hinged on terrible puns. Every single story made me think about my father. If Este had accused me of not wanting to be there tonight, I would have had to admit he was totally right.

"And now for the most chilling tale of all. What you're about to hear is one hundred percent true, and completely unsolved." The tour guide flipped his cape over one shoulder and waited for the crowd to draw near.

"In the summer of 1857, two children went missing. Mary Jones and Elijah Harper played together every day in front of Mary's father's store."

The guide whirled to the left and pointed at a building down the street. "The store was just over there, where the bank is today."

A few people took pictures, and one woman asked her companion if there were any orbs on the digital camera's display.

Jared rolled his eyes. "Oh come on," he said. "Not even the jackasses on *Ghost Hunters* take orbs seriously. I can't believe people are so dumb."

It wasn't aimed at me, but I felt defensive anyway. "Just because you don't believe in ghosts doesn't mean they don't exist."

"Uh huh," said Jared. "Sure."

The flurry of activity wound down, and the guide cleared his throat.

"Nine days and nights passed, and the children were given up for dead, but on the tenth day John Rowe found them on the docks when he went down to his fishing boat. Their hair had gone stark white, and they looked withered and old, like thinly veiled skeletons. It was as though for each day they'd been gone, a decade had passed. The children lived less than a week after that, and they never did say what happened."

The guide let his voice trail off into ominous silence for a few seconds, then banged his staff on the sidewalk once more and said, "This concludes our tour. Be sure to buy a copy of my book, *The Haunted History of St. John's*, with all of these stories and more!"

Our group scrambled to take photos with the guide and his flashing staff, but I hung back, thinking about my father, and about children growing old before their time. Then I looked up, and there he was. He stood in the shadows outside a circle of orange streetlight, his hands in his pockets with the knobs of his knuckles outlined under white linen. I could feel him watching me, slouching casually like he'd been there all night, waiting.

"Honey Baloney," he said.

"Why are you tormenting me?" I asked. "Can't you just leave me alone?"

My father smirked, the same full lips I have turning up at one side in an expression I knew I'd made a thousand times myself. He sketched a mocking half bow and stepped backward into the darkness.

*

After many hours of probing along the brown rock walls of New-foundland's eastern coast, Healuwo found a cave in which to rest. She could hear the outer edge of the thought cloud that was human existence, but didn't venture close enough to distinguish voices. She needed to think, and to go through her new cache of human things. She'd lucked into a good find while she was up at the surface recharging the tablet's solar battery. A boat, small and splintered, had capsized and gotten trapped between two sea boulders. There weren't a lot of exciting things, but she'd separated a small bit of netting to wear as decoration, one with a pretty green glass charm. It was, she thought, a good omen to finish her journey to human areas thus bejeweled.

It was an even better omen when she noticed the book floating nearby. The pages were almost too waterlogged to read, but any human text was worth trying to save. Healuwo had collected it carefully, using four arms to bring it close with the least amount of pressure, and progressed with painstaking care and slowness after that. Now that she had found shelter, she relaxed her grip ever so slightly, and with a fifth arm, shined the tablet's screen at her prize.

"...istory of St. John's"

It was an historical document, perfect preparation for her up-coming contact. Some of it was beyond salvation, but Healuwo was clever, and she didn't mind filling in the blanks. It was full of wonderful stories about how humans could continue in their humanity even after the corporeal phase had finished. The best piece, though, was about children who disappeared and grew old in a short time for humans.

The human document did not explain how this happened, but Healuwo knew the answer. These were surely some of the kings and queens of the underwater she'd so loved to hear about as a broodling. They went under the sea and became friends with all the people, learning the secrets of how to talk and breathe underwater. Some squid said those stories were untrue, but this proved otherwise. And if this was true, then her quest was not for nothing.

She settled in for her rest period with renewed hope. Soon she would take the next step. Soon she would find some human children of her own.

*

On our last day in Newfoundland, we went to Cape Spear, the easternmost point in North America. Kimberly took half of our party into the historic lighthouse, but Este kept Annie and Shane outside with the rest of us. There was a series of bunkers left over from World War II, which interested Jared and the kids particularly. Rusted, damp, and streaked with salt, they felt like sets from a video game. We took turns posing for pictures as zombie hunters, but my heart wasn't in it.

I hadn't seen my father since the night of the ghost tour, but I couldn't get him out of my mind. I didn't want to see him, but I couldn't keep from expecting it. It was like being twelve all over again, dreading his absence, and his return.

There must be unfinished business between us, I thought. That was always the way it worked in ghost stories. He wouldn't come back and talk to me without a reason. Would he?

This restless distraction drew me out of the bunkers and away from the group. I wanted to be alone. There was a busload of tourists on the main trail, so I veered onto a side path that led down the cliff side. It was probably a terrible idea, but I suddenly wanted very badly to touch the water.

About halfway to the bottom, I began to imagine a voice. Gentle as Consuela's whisper, it felt like it was coming from inside my own head. It spoke small encouragements to help me climb down.

By the time I reached the bottom, I had made up a whole story for the voice. It was a giant squid, lonely and benevolent, and we had moved on from encouraging remarks on my hiking skills to fantasies about escaping the drudgery of land life to live as a queen under the sea.

We can travel the world under the waves.

"Great," I said aloud, laughing at the surreal whims of my imagination. "But realistically, I could never leave Jared for a sea creature."

You're not young enough, the voice said sadly.

"Not young enough?" I asked, confused. The rest of it had seemed like a fanciful brain tangent, but this was different somehow.

I need the children, the voice said. *I'm bringing them down.*

Looking up, I saw two small figures starting down the cliffside path. They were too far away for me to recognize their faces, but I could see the colors of their clothes—one in lavender, the other in olive green—Annie and Shane. My breath caught in my throat, and my chest felt tight. Amusing daydreams were all well and good, but the reality of my brother's new stepchildren in danger? Not cool. I was all the way down by the water's edge, too far to reach them, even by shouting. I did the only thing I could think of.

"If you're real, and if you're luring children down a cliff, you need to stop," I said.

The voice that answered over the roar of the waves was not the one I expected. "Honey Baloney?"

I whipped around to see my father on a rocky outcropping several yards away. He wore the garish coral brocade suit that had always made Este and me embarrassed to be seen in public with him.

"I don't think you should be here," he said.

"What are you doing here?" I asked. Trust that he'd show up to complicate things at the worst possible time.

"I'm saving the children." He pointed to the cliff behind me. Annie and Shane were almost halfway down, both focusing with trance-like intensity. I knew their goal: touching water. Hadn't I had that same idea myself?

I looked back at my father, marveling at the vivid detail. His suit jacket flapped in the wind, and I could see the seams in the satin lining. His right hand gripped a spear with a nasty barbed head. I remembered all the violent stories from his drug trafficking years, feeling sick and angry. He'd always been unashamed of his crimes. He'd rationalized every horrible action and laughed at me for caring.

"You don't save people," I said. "You hurt them."

He didn't laugh now, though, which pissed me off even more.

"Why do you have a spear?" I demanded.

"Technically speaking, it's a harpoon," my father said, infuriating as always.

"What do you need a harpoon for?" I took a step toward him, thrusting my shoulders back, determined not to let him be the dominant one. Not this time.

He smiled, but it didn't reach his eyes. "There's a lot about me you don't know, Honey Baloney."

I didn't back down. Enough was enough. "What are you doing here? You were never around when I was a kid. Why am I seeing you now?"

"Trina, I love you. You'll always be my favorite daughter—"

"I'm your only daughter," I interrupted.

"Still," he said. "It's the truth. But you think everything is about you, and it isn't."

"What kind of answer is that?" I asked.

"You should go help them get back up," he said, pointing to the kids. "Be a good Auntie."

"Are *you* doing this to them? Who do you think you are to just show up like this and make trouble?"

My father shrugged. "Call me Ishmael," he said. Then he dove into the ocean.

I stood, mouth agape as his body disappeared under the water. A flash of red against his black dress shoes might have been the tip of a tentacle, or it might have just been a trick of the light on his gaudy suit.

Jared's shout from above jarred me out of my daze. He was

halfway down the cliff, hot on Annie and Shane's trail. Annie and Shane were already more than three quarters of the way down. I'd been so distracted by my father that I'd missed most of their descent.

"Stop," I called. "Don't move! I'm coming up to where you are."

I guess adrenaline made the climbing easier because it seemed like I reached them instantly. I grabbed their hands and held on tightly, carefully sitting us all down to wait for Jared. I wasn't about to try bringing them up without another adult to help.

"Why did you decide to climb down here on your own?" I asked.

Annie looked at me with serious grey eyes. "She said we could be king and queen under the sea."

"Who said?"

Shane scrunched up his face in confusion. "Don't know. She's not talking now."

"Because of Ishmael," Annie said, nodding. "He gets to be king instead."

I didn't know where to start untangling all the questions that came to mind when I heard that. Before I could even try, Jared came into earshot.

"Annie, Shane!" He called from a spot some twenty feet up. "What on Earth do you think you're doing? Este's going to kill me for letting you come down here."

I looked up, searching his face as he drew closer. He hadn't seen anyone else. I could tell. I would have to puzzle this out later, though. I stood, careful to keep myself between the kids and the steep drop. Jared held Shane's hand, and I held Annie's, and we all climbed up with painstaking slowness, grabbing onto jutting rocks to help us balance against the wind. By the time we reached the top, Este and a small crowd had gathered to receive us.

"What happened?" Este asked Jared. "I went to get a jacket from the car, and suddenly you were gone."

Jared shrugged sheepishly. "I swear I didn't look away for more than a second. They're wily little beasts. By the time I found them, they were halfway down the cliff."

The rest of the story tumbled out in confused chunks, everyone overlapping with clarifications and interjections. No one mentioned the strange voice, or my father, though.

Este pulled the kids close. "Thank God Tía Trina was there to stop you. Don't ever scare me like that again."

I wanted to tell him about what Annie and Shane had seen and heard, to make him reassure me that I wasn't crazy, but looking at the way they all clung to each other, I knew I couldn't. Not then. The echo of my father's voice lingered in my head. You think everything is about you, but it's not. He might have been a bastard, but sometimes he was right.

"You know what?" I said instead. "I think we all need some ice cream. Let's go find the others and get out of here."

Este took my hand and gave it a squeeze as we started walking toward the lighthouse. "Thanks," he said. "You know you're my favorite sister."

"I'm your only sister," I said.

"Still," said Este.

"Still," I agreed. "I'm glad I got stuck with you, too."

*

For the first while, Healuwo flushed with the pleasure of a task well-accomplished. She had not found children. She had found better. The man, the Ishmael, knew all about Captain Ahab. He carried a harpoon, and even if she could see he had no idea how to use it, even if the first Ishmael never used one anyway, it was the thought that counted. She could touch him. She could show him all the underwater places.

But soon her crimson faded to a demure rust. Always the guilt, always the remonstrance from Shaluraya and the others, bearing the echoes of their broodmother, who had died when they were still small ones. She was not behaving as a squid should. She was a discredit to her family. The knowledge itched and prickled like an urchin under her mantle.

Ishmael left for a few days—to find tribute, he said. He returned with a steak, which he claimed was whale, but which she knew was only tuna. He had not used the harpoon. She could sense the humanity on him. He had gone to the surface for it.

Why do you pretend? she asked. She was in between bites, her beak still half full of meat. Ishmael shuddered slightly when he looked at her, but he did not turn away.

What is truly troubling you? Ishmael asked. His eyes flashed sympathy and concern. He understood about the language of the sea. He did not need to breathe.

Healuwo didn't answer in words, but her agitated ripple showed well enough how she felt. Ishmael placed his soft human hands on the back of one of her arms, stroking down the length of it in a slow, firm gesture, and Healuwo calmed a bit in spite of herself.

The water is warmer in the South, said Ishmael. *I could show you my home as you have shown me yours.*

Healuwo curled two arms to cradle the place where she should have nourished a brood by now. *I have already displeased them so.*

Staying with family is optional, said Ishmael. *They will continue without you.*

Why do you stay with me?

Ishmael's hands stilled, and his mind closed as he sorted through his thoughts. She wished she could take the question back, was on the point of doing just that when Ishmael answered.

Apart, we might be monsters, whether we will it or not. He stroked her arm once more. *Together, we might do better.*

Healuwo considered this. She had never meant to hurt anyone. Not anyone human, anyway.

I will not brood if I go, she said. *Shaluraya would find that much worse than killing some divers.*

Another long, soothing stroke. *You do not wish to brood.*

No, Healuwo admitted.

The water is warmer in the South, Ishmael said again.

But what is in it for you?

Adventure, he said. *Homecoming. Tamarinds.*

Healuwo could feel her color strengthening already.

***

Julia Rios *is a writer, editor, podcaster, and narrator. She hosts the* Outer Alliance Podcast *(celebrating QUILTBAG speculative fiction), and is one of the three fiction editors at* Strange Horizons. *Her fiction, articles, interviews, and poetry have appeared in* Daily Science Fiction, Apex Magazine, Stone Telling, Jabberwocky, *and several other places. Visit her online at juliarios.com.*

Christmas Gifts

Timothy S. Kroecker

"Hello Mosk," the voice said from beside the poolside bar.

I froze. It had been forty years since I had spoken to Mother, but I'd have recognized that nails-on-chalk-board rasp if it had been a millennium. What was she doing at a remote resort in Punta Cana?

"Wow! That's Glo!" the young bride whispered to her husband, pointing up at Mother.

I focused on the honeymoon couple, placed my palms on their arms and locked their attention on me. My mother's laugh made me tighten my grip harder than I'd intended. I eased the pressure and drew a small amount of their life-energy into me. Even if they were only small-time marks, I did like them both and this way, Mother would never take from them. She wasn't the sort to settle for sloppy seconds.

"So should I book you for the sailing trip tomorrow?" I wanted the fat commission from the yacht's Captain and smiled at their vague nods. "Excellent!" Still refusing to acknowledge my mother's presence, I sent a last pulse of pleasure through the couple. "Judging from how *happy* Brad is, we probably won't see you until tomorrow."

Brad, a professional football player, wasn't embarrassed by his obvious excitement. He guffawed and drew his plastic-surgery perfect wife close. She giggled and they walked up the beach and the pristine pathway that wound among the manicured trees back to their suite. They would make frantic love and fall into an exhausted sleep that would last until the morning, due more to my feeding than their frenetic activities. I'd have to remember to have the front desk wake them up in time for the trip.

Steeling my expression, I faced the woman who had so reluctantly given birth to me nearly ninety years ago. I stayed my ground and let her come to me. I wanted to watch her and assess where she was in her cycle.

She looked different than I remembered, but that didn't surprise me—in between her fall and rise, her appearance always changed. Before me stood a woman in her early twenties. Her white bikini set off her mocha-toned skin perfectly. She had a curvaceous body with full, rounded breasts. Beautifully coiffed brown hair wrapped around her head like a crown. Designer sunglasses hid her eyes. Her measured pace reminded me of a lioness stalking its prey. She might still be in ascent, when she was at her most attractive, talented, and still toying with her entourage.

"You didn't need to send your precious tidbits away, Mosk. I've brought my buffet with me," she said and looked back up the pathway to the pool. There were two large, muscular men carefully watching over her. If I made a wrong move, two handguns would be pointed at me in a split second. It would take more than that to kill me, but it certainly wouldn't be a pleasant experience.

"They're newlyweds. They were just on their way back to their room," I told her.

The way she looked up the pathway after the couple made me uncomfortable. Just because she said she wouldn't feed off them didn't mean she wouldn't hurt them out of spite. She reached up to touch the white ball on the tip of my Santa cap but I jerked away from her.

"What are you doing here, Moth?" I asked, deliberately using the nickname she hated. When she emerged from wherever she hid herself after her falls, she flitted back toward fame like a moth to a flame and always with the same result. Her smile faded and she took her sunglasses off.

"I am Glo now," she said proudly. "My videos are viral and seen around the world. I have more money and power from this single incarnation than your measly gifts could accrue over centuries," she said, again moving closer, trying to provoke me. If I struck her, the guards would riddle me with bullets.

I smiled at her. She could never understand how much control I had over my instincts because she had none. As she approached I looked at her eyes. The red streaks around her pupils, the fine lines in the corners of her eyes, and the way her gaze darted around meant she was just past her zenith. Her slide down wasn't far off.

I glanced up at her guards, this time feeling sympathy rather than fear. The casual and minor incidents of violence that surrounded Mother would soon turn deadly for all of her inner circle and their families. While ascending, she took care of them and fattened them like livestock. In descent, she fed.

"How did you find me and what do you want?" I asked.

"One of my cattle was here on vacation some time ago. She told me about a cheerful, ebony-skinned man who made people happy with his singing, smiles, and hugs. I knew it had to be you," she said, and then added as an afterthought, "Can't a mother want to see her son?"

"Not you, Moth. Never you," I said.

"I'll kill you if you call me that again," she snarled, leaning forward. I bared my teeth right back at her but said nothing, trying to avoid provoking either of us any further. Her guards moved down the pathway but she waved them off.

"You can have the hotel if that's what you want. I'll move on. I've been here too long anyway," I told her, willing to cede it to her rather than risk drawing attention. My gifts weren't like hers; I couldn't survive an intense level of scrutiny. I turned away from her and the hotel.

"Wait." She paused a long moment. "Please." Her tone slowed my step. I heard a sincere plea in her voice.

"What?" I asked.

"I need your help."

What could I do for her that she couldn't do more efficiently and ruthlessly herself? Now I turned to her, my hand resting on the back of a wooden lounge chair.

"Your gift," she answered my unspoken question. "I want to let one of my cattle go more easily. Without the usual pain and insanity." Her tone was soft, uncomfortable. An image of Abuela, my grandmother, came to mind. In it, her eyes were pleading rather than stern. I pushed the memory away, not wanting to be vulnerable in front of Mother.

56

There was a loud crack. I looked down, realizing I had broken the wooden plank at the top of the lounge chair.

"Never, Mother. And don't try to find me again. I've had years to plan how to disappear when I need to. You won't be able to find me. Especially while you're in descent."

I had enough cash to get out of the Dominican Republic and establish a new identity in Jamaica or one of the other islands within days. I turned away from her again and made it half way up the pathway the newlyweds had taken before she spoke again.

"Abuela would want you to do this," she said quietly, knowing I could hear her. I stopped. Mother and I had nothing in common except our love for Abuela. I was no saint. I had killed to protect my secret when an unsavory nun had found me out. But I did try to use my gifts in secret to ease pain and suffering when I could. Mother loved no one, not me, not even herself at her nadir. She did nothing that didn't benefit her. Abuela was the only exception I knew of in all of Mother's long series of lives.

"I hate you, Moth," I said.

"No less than I hate you, Mosquito," she replied.

"Meet me here at dawn tomorrow. If I have to stay another moment this close to you, I will kill you."

I could hear her laughing at me as I walked up the pathway towards the hotel lobby.

What did Mother really want? I couldn't believe she sought me out to help one of her flock. Especially now, so close to the height of her cycle. They still loved her. They still wanted to be with her. She was still basking in their attention and affection.

*

Mother remained in her private cottages with her entourage during the festivities held that and each night at the hotel. I didn't see any of them and they would be easy for me to spot. They would be beautiful. "Great chefs care about presentation," Mother used to say, referring to her "food." Her people's partying would be desperate and intense. They didn't know Mother had her hooks into them, siphoning their energy and emotions and slowly pushing them to extremes of drugs and violence, squeezing their life forces out of them.

I left the other workers to clean up after the evening limbo contest and said one last lingering lucrative goodbye to the wealthier guests before making my way to the employee parking lot. Besides the hotel's manager, I was the only employee with my own transportation. He had an old Honda Civic. While I could afford any luxury car I wanted, I kept a low profile by owning a pasola, a small motorbike. Unlike Mother, I didn't crave material things for attention or status nor did my finances spike high or crash low. They grew at a steady pace in a variety of banks, investment accounts, and safety deposit boxes in the Caribbean, and in Central and South America.

The drive to my latest apartment helped to soothe the nerves Mother had frazzled. There were few other people on the road that late. For the first five minutes I drove along manicured entrances to other high-end resorts along the beach, passing only the occasional taxi, returning early from the nightclubs. After the resorts came the vacation mansions belonging to rich Americans, Canadians, or Dominicans from Santo Domingo. If I was more like Mother, I would live in one of them but Abuela had taught me better. "Live quietly, stay hidden, blend in when you can," she'd said.

As I got closer to the town, the number of homes along the roadside increased. Many had windows lit with Christmas lights. I passed several local bars that had drinking, laughing people at the tables. One of the things I loved most about Dominicans—they were always happy and ready to party.

I drove the motorbike up to my side street and killed the engine. In the distance I could hear music from the discos and nightclubs. The tourist bars would be full of rich people. Since I was probably leaving town, I decided I would go out again a little later. I could use the extra cash and energy.

Walking the bike made me feel vulnerable but it was late and I knew the neighbors would not appreciate the noise. Most of them were educated professionals with day jobs that started early. As I pulled up to the steps leading to my second-story apartment, I saw a woman sitting there. For a split second I thought it was Mother again but then I recognized her as the woman from the first floor apartment. It was very late for her to be up and out.

The woman, dressed in a t-shirt and cotton pajama bottoms, looked up at me as I approached. Her apartment door, next to the stairway, was ajar. The light from the Christmas tree inside let me see that she was crying.

"Señora, is everything okay? It's late," I asked, knowing it would be expected of me. Abuela's lessons had, over the long years, become habit.

"Buenas noches, Señor. I'm sorry. Let me get out of your way," she said, ignoring my question and standing. I had to bring the motorbike inside my apartment or it wouldn't be there in the morning. As I manhandled it up the steps I could hear a child moaning. I didn't have any children—I couldn't sire them—but I'd lived long enough to know she was crying in pain.

"Señora, what's wrong?"

She brushed the hair from in front of her red and swollen eyes. Taking a hitched breath, she said, "It's my niña, Ana. She went for a treatment today. The pain won't let her sleep or rest. I don't know what to do!" She started crying again.

"I'm so sorry. I didn't know she was ill," I said. It wasn't true, but it sounded more sympathetic than the truth. "Have you tried warm milk?" I could feel Abuela's disapproving eyes on me like old times. We both knew I could help the situation.

"No! I should have thought of that! Ana likes milk. Maybe that will help! Thank you!" she said smiling faintly.

She wiped her eyes and hugged the building's wall to let me pass. I shrunk as far from her as I could. I didn't want to feed off the neighbors, even by accident. It would lead to problems.

She was about to say more but Ana's cries started up again. She looked at me quickly and then went into her apartment, closing the door behind her. I unlocked the door to my apartment and brought the motorbike inside. After I closed the door, I was still able to hear Ana crying.

I leaned the bike against the wall and flipped on the living room light. Cool and detached as a hotel room, there were no decorations or personal items inside, only beige and neutral-toned furniture. I went into my bedroom, turned on the light, and slid a suitcase from beneath the bed. There was little to pack but I put my favorite shirts and pants into the case along with some toiletries. Lastly, I picked up the old and battered frame sitting on the dresser. In it, a middle-aged, dark-skinned woman dressed in her Sunday best looked out at me from a sepia-toned photograph.

Abuela wasn't Mother's mother, she was at least a century younger than Mother. Abuela had taken her in after finding her wondering the street, filthy, deranged, pregnant with me, and at the bottom of one of her worst cycles. Abuela had a big heart, had been a strict Catholic, and was the only person other than me immune to Mother's poisonous charisma. Abuela helped Mother give birth to me, accepted her physical changes at the beginning of her cycle, and drove her out when it was clear I wasn't safe with Mother around. Abuela never judged either one of us despite our parasitic natures—she left that up to God—but did discourage the worst of our impulses.

Abuela's smile seemed more strained than I remembered. Ana's cries grew louder—she must be in the room right below me. Abuela's eyes behind the smile reprimanded me. I sighed.

"Are you haunting me now as well as Mother?" I asked. I turned away from her and left my apartment, slamming the front door behind me, resenting the conscience she had given me.

I stomped down the stairs and knocked on the first floor apartment door. I waited a few moments and knocked again, louder. The woman answered the door, her eyes red and puffy.

"I'm sorry about the noise, Señor. I'm trying to get Ana to sleep.

"Oh no, Señora. Ana's cries break my heart. I am sometimes able to help my nieces and nephews get to sleep when I sing to them." She looked at me dubiously. "Is she still in pain?"

I reached out to her. She took my hand without thinking and I drew some energy from her despite my rule against doing so. I gave her a quick pulse of pleasure. "It can't hurt," I said. "I'm not that bad a singer!"

I laughed and gave her another pulse. I didn't want to waste too much of my time here.

"Well, I guess it can't. Come in." She relented and stepped aside. Her husband was sitting on the couch. A young girl, about ten years old sat on his lap, crying and squirming feebly. She looked wan and pale. The man looked exhausted but was trying to distract his daughter by pointing and talking about the Christmas tree. He looked a question at his wife.

"It's the man from upstairs. He says he might be able to sing Ana to sleep."

"I'm an entertainer at the resorts," I explained to his puzzled frown. He looked at his daughter and again at his wife and shrugged.

"Anything is worth a try at this point. Come in," he said wearily, leaning back into the couch. Across from the couch was a coffee table. I sat carefully on it and leaned toward Ana. She hadn't opened her eyes since the door opened.

"Hello, Dulcita," I said and brushed her forehead with the palm of my hand. I drew a small trickle of energy from her. It told me she was very ill and not likely to live many more weeks. I gave her a pulse of pleasure. She opened eyes that were sunken and shadowed.

"Can I sing you a song? It may help you go to sleep," I said.

"Can I go to bed? Pappy isn't as comfortable as the bed. And he's too hot. Sorry, Pappy," she said with an apologetic, thin, smile. He laughed quietly and stood with her in his arms.

"Let's go, niña. It's good to see you smile." He smiled gratefully at me and gestured with his head to follow him; his wife right behind me. My steps slowed as we entered Ana's room. There were two posters on the wall; both were of Glo.

"Ana loves Glo, don't you niña?" her mother asked from behind me. I tried, with only marginal success, to turn my grimace into a smile when I saw Ana's father looking at me. He leaned down and put Ana in her bed as his wife moved to lower the sheets and fuss with the pillows. Ana smiled and nodded wearily but looked at the posters with adoration in her eyes.

Ana looked at me expectantly. I looked at them all with a wide, disarming smile and sat on the edge of her bed. I took the girl's hand in mine and saw a Glo doll on the little table next to her bed. Still smiling, I turned my body so I couldn't see the doll or either of the posters. I sang two songs and drew as little energy from her as possible while sending slow waves of pleasure through her, blocking her pain. By the end of the second song her breathing had deepened and she was asleep.

"Thank you!" Ana's mother whispered.

I stood up and moved quickly to the front door, anxious to be away but my thoughts lingered on Ana and Mother.

"Thank you," she said again. Before I could avoid it, she had me in a tight hug. For a split second I resisted but then hugged her back, touching my cheek to hers. Next to my hands, my face and lips were the best for drawing energy and transmitting the pleasure that I could offer in payment. With Abuela on my mind, I sent a pulse of pleasure into the woman, hoping she would be able to rest. I did the same to her husband when he pumped my hand. I bid them good night and made empty promises when they insisted I stop by on Christmas day.

I ran back to my apartment, quickly showered, and changed

my clothes. In less than ten minutes, I was ready to hit the bars to suck more energy and money from hapless tourists.

*

As Christmas Eve day arrived, I went back to my apartment and showered, getting ready for my job and my meeting at dawn with Mother. It had been a great night. I was gifted a great deal more money and several gold chains. I'd have to make another trip to one of my safe deposit boxes soon. Or perhaps I could use the gold to bribe a new identity from a minor official in another country. It would be an option if Mother made the hotel her home for the next few months.

I jumped on my motorbike and drove back to the resort. The roads were more crowded now with buses full of returning hotel employees. As I drove up the winding driveway to the resort, I passed two of the buses chugging their way up the hill. The day was already hot and the buses were packed. Two young men eyed me jealously from the back of one bus. I grinned at them then laughed when they made a rude gesture.

"You're late," Mother said from a beach chair, hidden behind a large umbrella. Her voice was gravelly and raspy – not a good sign.

"It's dawn. I'm on the beach. What do you want?" I asked, ignoring her barb.

"Your gift, I told you."

"I have many gifts. I can sing. I can dance. I've been told I play the piano very well. Do you want me to play while you sing?"

"Stop being an idiot. I need the one gift you have that could be of any use to anyone. The one you used to kill Abuela."

I answered her quietly; looking around to make sure no one

else was near. "She was dying. I made it painless for her." I defended myself from her and an old guilt.

"You still took her life force," she answered me, in a loud tone, deliberately ignoring my hint not to draw attention to us.

"That's the way it works. If I could have given her some of my life force, or better yet, yours, I would have." I knew I should walk away, but I had to know what her game was this time.

"Who do you need it for?" I walked around the umbrella to see her face when she answered. I took satisfaction that she looked awful—her eyes were even more bloodshot and sunken. The wrinkles around her lips were more pronounced. This descent and crash were likely to be spectacular.

"His name is Charlie. He's like Abuela. My gifts don't affect him. He's been with me a long time." I looked at her incredulously. "He has colon cancer. He asked me to bring him here to die."

I blinked. I hadn't thought Mother was capable of caring for anything—even herself—especially after she began her descent. I paused and thought about her request. I had killed with my gift only twice in my life—one was Abuela, the other a woman in the prime of her life who hid her greed, ambition, and sadism behind a religious habit. Both times I felt the pull of death, a tug on my own life force that awoke in me a morbid curiosity about what lay on the other side of the veil. That fascination frightened me more than anything else, even Mother.

"He'll have to tell me that's what he wants. I'm not a cold-blooded killer," I told her, hoping he had no idea about my gifts or the ability to voice his wishes. But I knew I would help him if he asked, if he could resist Mother's gifts and still love her, he earned an easier passing. She snorted at my words.

"He will," she assured me. Then she narrowed her eyes, surprised I agreed so easily. "What do you want?" I thought about the answer for a moment, considered telling her I wanted to meet someone as special as Abuela again, get a glimpse of that time when I felt less alone, less damned, but I shook my head, knowing she would only use it against me.

I smiled. "A signed copy of your latest CD, and autographed photo—made out to Ana, and one of your dolls in the original boxes, also signed."

"That's it?" she asked, frowning. I nodded but another idea began to take shape.

"Wait. There's more."

She smiled, more comfortable with a response she could understand. "What do you want?"

"Only a few moments of your time," I said, not willing to say more. "Come to my apartment building tomorrow and be as charming and beguiling as you were at your apex."

Her eyes turned feral. "I am not one of my dolls. Don't tell me what to do. No one does—ever."

"There's a little girl. She's dying. Charlie will want you to do what I ask of you." I enjoyed turning the ploy she used on me against her.

The mention of Charlie brought sanity back to her eyes.

"When do you want me to talk to Charlie?"

"The drugs aren't helping anymore no matter how much we give him," Mother said, telling me more than she realized. One of her cattle could kill the man but it would be brutal and painful. That was the way she normally liked it. "I've said my good-byes already. I'll have one of my cattle bring your payment."

She walked quickly past me but not so fast that I didn't spot the tears running down her cheeks.

I took another path to the suite of rooms she had booked and knocked softly on Charlie's door, entering when a barely audible voice answered. On the bed, half under the covers lay a cadaverously thin white man. He peered at me through blue, filmy, sunken eyes.

"You Mosquito?" he asked, speaking was obviously difficult and painful. I nodded. He coughed softly, grimacing. Only days or hours remained of his life and it would only bring agony as his body corroded.

"What do you want me to do?"

"Come closer," he said.

I sat next to him on the chair by the bed. He reached out and grabbed my hand, surprising me.

"You're so much like her, and yet so different" he said, staring at my eyes. I looked away.

My thoughts paralleled his—he was so much like her—like Abuela, yet different. His touch made me feel calm, centered. Just like hers had. I wished Mother had called me sooner so that I could have known more of him.

"What do you want me to do?" I asked

"Help me die in peace. Please." The last word was a whisper, trailing off as a wave of pain crossed his face. I waited until it passed and he could look at me again.

"Now?" He nodded. I sat down next to him on the bed, saying nothing as I placed my hand on his forehead. Immediately I could feel his illness, his life force tainted by the cancer. I sent a strong pulse of pleasure coursing down my hand. Within seconds the worst of the tension eased from his body and his face relaxed. He flashed a hopeful look at me. "The feeling won't last very long. I'm sorry." The glow faded. "I can make it painless and quick. Do you want me to continue?" He took a deep breath which I kept free of coughing and looked at me again.

"She has good in her," he said quietly, speaking of Mother. "I wasn't strong enough to make her see it. But, you could."

I pulled my hand back. He didn't know the horrors that had been done because of her. That she had done. She could never change.

"Please," he said, "Your Abuela knew the truth. I can tell you know it too. Show her for me. I love her." I cringed at another request in Abuela's name.

He took my hand and placed it on his forehead again. "Now." he said. "Please." I nodded again and put my other hand on his skeletal shoulder. With one hand I sent another wave of pleasure through his system and drew his pitiful life force out with the other. As it trailed off, I felt that odd feeling as if there was someone on the other side who in turn began pulling my life force toward them. Fearfully, I resisted the strange impulse to let my draining happen and finished taking Charlie's. It was over within seconds. After I closed his eyes, I left the room as quietly as I had entered.

*

The next morning, at exactly 9:00am, Mother pulled up in a limousine and stepped out onto the sidewalk in all her Glo-glory. Ana was sitting on the steps with me and her parents. Her eyes sparkled and a smile lit her face. "Glo!"

She stood weakly and hugged Mother before I could think to stop her.

Mother looked at me over the tops of her sunglasses. She gave a wide, false smile to Ana's parents but I could see the anger and insanity simmering behind it. I had no idea what she would do next.

"Preciosa," she said, "do not exert yourself so." She carefully pried Ana away and set her on the steps and covered the moment by tenderly pushing Ana's hair from her face. Ana beamed.

Mother walked to stand in front of me and gave me a Hollywood-style air kiss.

"I came," she whispered.

I stood and whispered in her ear. "This is Ana. She loves you. Give her the doll." I pointed to where I had put them on the stairway above us. "Tell her you love her and you hope she gets well soon. That's it."

She smirked, thinking me foolish for wasting her favor. I could see the wheels in her mind spinning, planning some way to turn this against me.

"Do it for Charlie, not me," I coaxed her quietly, remembering his request to show Mother another way. Perhaps this would be the first step.

That night I unpacked my bag, ignoring the hint of a smile I saw on Abuela's picture, and readied myself to go out and replenish my energy from the seasonal tourists.

***

Timothy S. Kroecker *is a psychologist working for the U.S. Air Force. He grew up reading fantasy and science fiction and worked in a library while going through college. Tim enjoys writing urban fantasy and young adult fiction. Tim and his wife share their home with three miniature schnauzers and more than eight hundred frogs they've collected over the years.*

The Doorway

E.L. Mellor

A young thief grabbed my satchel of herbs as I walked home from the Burmister's house on a damp evening in early spring. I cursed my ears for not hearing him creep up behind as I chased him down the street and into a blind alley, my stride hampered by skirts. Halfway to the town wall, I nearly caught him, but suspicion slowed my steps. The postern at alley's end had been locked shut for as long as anyone could remember, so where did he think he was going? A stranger might not realize there was no way out through the east wall, but a lad his age should have easily outpaced a woman four decades older. I stopped.

He kept running. Light from a moon nearly full angled into the space between stucco walls, streaking silver in the dark hair that flew out behind him. The boy paused and looked back for a moment before he reached the wooden door, then seemed to run straight through it. I thought it must be a trick of the moonlight or my dimming eyes, that he'd simply withdrawn to one of the shadowed corners on either side. No thief's escape, then, but a trap for an old woman.

I backed out, keeping my hand on the knife at my belt until I reached my shop and barred the door behind me, where the familiar scent of herbs and old wood slowed the race of my heart. Never one to cower from a blow, I'd fended off thieves in the past but could no longer deny my waning strength. Long afterward I lay awake in the chamber above, still burning at the loss of my satchel.

Yet I'd known more dire losses through the years, and this one, at least, could be set right. The thief had not taken the Burmister's coin, kept safe in a pocket beneath my skirt, and Mirek the shoemaker would sew me a new satchel for a fair price. I fell asleep breathing the lavender that hung from the beams overhead.

A dream took me back to the alley. I saw a door shining in the light of a full moon, flanked on either side by my grandmother and the old woman who'd held the shop before me. My Babka stood tall and straight as I remembered her, the bones of her face in fierce outline beneath sunbrowned skin, crowned with a silver braid. A head shorter, Yaja the herbalist appeared as I'd only heard others describe her, a softly rounded old woman with shrewd eyes and a crooked smile.

My heart filled with sorrow that I'd never repaid them for their gifts. I yearned to run to them, to give the thanks I'd forgotten when young, but, in the way of dreams, my legs felt stone heavy and moved as slowly. The women joined hands across the door, as if to bar my way, and faded to mist before I could reach them.

*

The pungent sweetness of steeping aniseed filled the shop next morning as I checked my stores of herbs and unguents. A pain stabbed the back of my knee, no doubt from running after the boy, while the dream haunted my thoughts.

Years had passed since I'd recalled the week spent with Yaja. When I wandered into her shop seeking work, she was not merely old and worn, like my Babka before she died, but a decrepit ruin of a woman. Her withered flesh had sagged from its bones like wax on a candle, and the odor of decay followed her painful steps when she made the effort to rise from her bed.

A girl had arrived in town a month or so before I did, claiming to be Yaja's niece summoned from the countryside to nurse her through an illness. She looked enough like the herbalist that no one doubted her story, although Yaja had seemed hearty as ever when last seen. After several weeks of keeping the shop and giving polite answers to all who asked after her aunt, she vanished overnight.

The wife of the shoemaker across the street had found Yaja trembling on a pallet in the kitchen behind the shop, unable to climb the stairs to her bedchamber and looking as if she'd aged a hundred years. Some suggested the girl had poisoned her to steal what coin she'd saved, but the old woman met questions with silence, saying only, "She won't return." When I appeared the next day asking for work, her neighbors reacted with wariness to the arrival of a second strange girl. Although my clothes and hair were filthy from sleeping on the ground during my journey, Yaja wouldn't let them throw me out. She insisted on hearing how much I knew of herbs and where I came by my knowledge.

After I told her what my grandmother had taught me, she said to the shoemaker's wife, "The girl knows enough to be of use, and I need a nurse. Let her stay with me, and you can go back to your own work."

I cared for her as well as I could, while the women on the street visited and brought food, but nothing I knew or Yaja suggested helped in the least. Desperate with both sympathy for the old woman and fear of losing my place, I asked if there were anything more I might try. Yaja said there was only one thing left to do—I should bring a man of law, and she would deed her shop to me, if I promised to sell herbs and remedies to the townspeople in her place.

"They need my herbs, and I abandoned them," she whispered in her broken voice.

"You couldn't help getting ill."

"I should have chosen an apprentice—a few quick-witted girls asked—but I could never bear seeing someone young about the place."

The vanished girl had clearly not taken the herbalist's stash of coins, as some claimed, since Yaja paid the man of law with a few and gave me the rest. She told me to buy a good woolen gown and order a new pair of shoes from the shoemaker, Mirek's father.

"And keep your hair neatly braided. People will trust you better if you look prosperous and respectable. They'll need time to accept a stranger in the shop, and a young one at that."

I overheard Yaja's last words to the shoemaker's wife, "I paid my own price." A day later, the townspeople carried her out to the graveyard beyond the postern in the west wall.

It never crossed my mind at sixteen that I might not know enough to carry on in the herbalist's stead. Having made what I thought a clever escape from the manor where my mother had bound me to work, I felt equal to any challenge. The plague years had taught me otherwise, of course, but the afterglow of that sun-lit bravado bore me through dark hours.

Once the aniseed syrup had cooled, I poured it into flasks to replace what I'd lost with the stolen satchel. The town saw a lot of croup in the chill of early spring.

*

That afternoon, Mirek stepped from his shop across the street as I set out for the market square to buy more honey. He and his granddaughter went instead of his daughter, since Leshka was so close to her time.

I told Mirek of the boy who stole my satchel, as Bozhena looked over the first greens of spring at a farmer's stall.

"A stranger?" he asked.

"I've never seen him before. Either he didn't know there was no way out through that postern or he's so new to town he mistook the east wall for the west."

"What did he look like?"

"Near my height, maybe fifteen or sixteen years. Pale, dark-haired, slender. Too pretty."

Mirek laughed. He knew I'd never had much time for men. "Like Tomaszek?"

The blacksmith's handsome son had most of the town's girls and a few of the boys hanging out of windows to watch him pass when his father sent him on errands. A boyhood spent wielding bellows and hammer had added sinew to height, and his skin glowed rosy bronze.

"No, not like Tomaszek. This boy looked as if he'd hardly worked a day in his life, though he wore the clothes of a laborer."

Bozhena picked out the freshest bundle of greens on the table and haggled over the price. Mirek paid the farmer, then said, "I'll cut out a new satchel as soon as I can get leather at the tanner's. The wine merchant's shoes need to be finished, and Leshka may not be able to work much for a while, but if you don't mind Stash doing the stitching, you can have it in a week or two."

As we walked back to our street, I asked Bozhena. "Will you follow your brother into the trade?"

"No. My Jadek says I haven't the knack for leatherwork, but now that I help keep the house, Matka can make more shoes."

*

The Burmister's infant boy wheezed with croup for a second night, while a little girl near the south gate burned in a fever, so I packed aniseed syrup and herbs in a small scrip which I held close. The full moon lit my walk back to the shop. When soft footsteps began to follow mine along the street, I pulled out my knife and turned to find the boy behind me.

"What do you want? You already have my satchel."

His eyes glittered in the moonlight as he approached, looking me up and down with the same sort of lewd stare I'd gotten a month or so before from an old vagabond who'd staggered into my shop. My life had not left me ignorant of the desires of men, but this shook me. I was old enough to be the boy's *babka*.

He whispered, "You're still a fine-looking woman. I wish I'd known you when you were young. Come with me!"

At that moment, Mirek called from his doorway, "Felcha, is all well?"

The boy fled toward the alley, Mirek and I following. We watched him run toward the postern, and, once again, he seemed to disappear. When we reached it, Mirek's lantern shone into empty angles.

"It looked like he ran straight through," he said, as he held the light higher.

I trailed the tips of my fingers over the door. For the few inches lit only by the lantern, it felt as wood always did to me, alive with the sun and warmth of summers long past. When I reached the moonlit strip at its center, my two longest fingers sank in slightly, as if the boards were rotting fruit that only looked sound. I pulled my hand back as from a flame.

We turned and left the alley in silence. My fingertips burned, while fear wrapped itself around my heart, as it seldom had since the plague. Mirek waited for me to enter at my door and bar it before he crossed the street to his own. We said nothing more than good night—for what could we say?—but his deep voice made a blessing of it, which I carried upstairs. My fingers still felt as if they'd touched fire. Sleep took its time, and in my dreams every path led to the moonlit door.

*

Sunlight leaking through the shutters woke me early next morning. Glad to find my fingertips no longer burned, I held my left hand up to the light. It was brown on the back, red on the palm, hardened by a half-century and more of work—all but the tips of the two inmost fingers, which now felt soft and smooth, their nails perfect ovals. Even at sixteen I didn't have such hands; work had roughened them long before I was grown.

How could a boy run through a door? How had my fingers sunk into solid wood and been so changed? Half-remembered tales of magic flitted through my mind. Perhaps the postern had been cursed in some way. And I wondered about the beautiful boy. Was he a sorcerer? Or one of the demons priests warned of? No ordinary boy of his years would speak to an old woman as he had to me.

While it was still early, I went across to Mirek's shop to show him my hand and ask what he thought. Because I found him leaving to fetch the midwife for his daughter, I said nothing but that I would bring chamomile and wormwood to ease her labor.

"Leshka thinks Bozhena's young yet to attend the birth and hopes she can stay with you," Mirek told me as he left.

Bozhena stomped into my shop a short while later, bearing a basket with greens, turnips, and a piece of pork.

"Matka said I can sit with Jadek and Stash in the shop or come here, so I'm going to cook stew for us all," she said, in a tone that made clear how offended she was at being sent away.

She asked for fennel seed and juniper berries, then wanted to know which barrel held kasha and whether I had an onion. As the stew simmered on the fire, she went to the baker in the next lane for rye loaves. Bozhena took a share to the midwife in late morning, then called her grandfather and brother to my table. It was a rare blessing not to have make my own dinner, and the girl did know how to cook. We all talked and laughed as we ate.

After Mirek and Stash returned to their leatherwork, Bozhena offered to help in the shop. She'd been in and out of my door almost since she could walk, always asking what lovage tasted like or what elecampane might be good for. Sometimes she helped me gather from field and wood those plants that didn't grow in my small patch outside the town walls, although Bozhena's housekeeping duties had kept her home more since her father's death that winter.

"How old were you when your father died?" she asked, as we stripped dried rosemary leaves from stems.

"About twelve."

"What happened to you after that?"

"My Babka and I gathered herbs to sell along with the remedies we made from them until she died two years later, when I was about Stash's age. Then my mother sent me to work as a servant for a *pan* and *pani* on a manor, and I was allowed to walk home once a month to bring her my wages."

Bozhena looked more curious. "How did you come here?"

"After two years I took my month's wages and ran away, then walked for three or four days to reach a market town far enough from the manor that I wouldn't be found. I asked for an herbalist who might want a helper and found old Yaja dying without an apprentice. She left the shop to me."

I didn't tell Bozhena that I had run, in part, because the father and son of the manor had begun trying to catch me alone. The boy I could duck or swat, but when illness kept the lady of the household in her bed, the man began to grab at me and demand that I meet him at night. Telling my mother would have been of no use, since she wanted my wages, and I knew I could not avoid the *pan* much longer.

"Did you ever have a husband?"

"No. I made my way alone." I'd also refused the other choice my mother offered, to marry an old farmer with two wives buried.

We talked of herbs until Stash came in midafternoon to say the baby had been born, and they left to see their new sister. I'd almost forgotten about my fingers. No one else had noticed them, but their wrongness left me uneasy, and they made the rest of me seem older. It struck me more keenly how my hands had begun to stiffen and my legs to ache on cold mornings.

*

Late that night when all was quiet, and I thought Mirek would not be keeping watch, I walked to the alley as the first moonbeam touched the door in the east wall. I was neither surprised nor frightened to hear the boy creep up behind me a third time.

"So you've come," he said. "I knew you would. When the door's full lit, go through and you'll be made young again."

Had I not seen my fingers sink into the wood and lose all signs of their years, I would have called him mad and fled. Instead, I waited.

As the bar of moonlight on the door widened, I thought of what I might do with my old strength revived. From time to time I glanced at the boy. "I want to see you beautiful," he said from the other side of the alley, where he leaned against the wall.

No one who knew me would have tried to tempt me in such a way. At sixteen I'd looked like any healthy young girl, with shining hair and pink cheeks, but had never been accused of possessing beauty, nor had I cared enough how men saw me to feel much grief for what I'd lost. Youth was no lure; death I feared not at all.

Only the thought of lingering in the world too weak to work frightened me. I wanted never to become as frail and helpless as Yaja when I met her.

We watched together, beautiful boy and old woman, as moonlight crept across the door, until most of it shone silver. Yet still I hesitated, wary.

"Go now," he urged.

I remembered how Babka and Yaja had seemed to bar my way in the dream.

"What is the cost?" I asked.

"Well," he said, after a long pause, "it feels like you're on fire when you pass through, and I think you must go through at every full moon to keep the change. A month ago, I stumbled down the alley one night and leaned against the door. I fell into a faint thinking I was burning alive, only to awaken on the ground outside the wall next morning, looking as you see me."

"Where did you go? You haven't been in town."

"Out to the countryside. Plenty of farmers will hire a boy for the spring planting, even a thin one, provided he can work. I returned with a month's wages to buy clothes that weren't in tatters and to look for you."

I stepped back a pace, not liking the way he eyed me. "I've never had much time for men—nor boys, either, even pretty ones."

He smiled in disbelief. "You'll feel different once you're made young. Go now," he said again. "It only works for the three nights around the full moon. When light fades from the planks, it will be an ordinary door again."

Might I have found a way to hold on to my strength so I'd never need to lean on anyone? Then I thought of my shop. What would people say when I appeared with a smooth face and dark braids again? The priests would no doubt hear of it, and I'd have to leave town, work, friends—the life I'd built over forty years. The price to regain what I'd lost would be all I still had.

The alley was a dead end, a trap for an old woman.

When I turned to leave, he came a few paces nearer and seized my arm. I recoiled and pulled away, not so much out of fear as from the smell of him. He gave off the stench of a dying old man, or maybe a three-day corpse. Worse than that, for in the presence of the sick or dead I felt no more than natural disgust, while this caused the blood to pound in my head and my heart urged me to run as far and fast as I was able from both him and the door. His smell also seemed somehow familiar, and I strove to remember where I'd met it before.

The force with which I'd wrenched myself from his grasp left the boy stunned for a few moments, but he soon came at me again, desperation contorting his face until he looked almost like one of the gargoyles on the church roof. "You must go with me!"

"That's why you took my satchel? To lead me through the door after you?"

"I can't keep this shape otherwise. I don't want to be old and sick. I don't want to die." Tears trickled from his eyes.

My revulsion grew. This was no sorcerer or demon, just a feeble old man desperate to regain his youth. "How do you know you need to bring someone through?"

"I felt myself growing weaker as the moon waxed, just before I came back to town. I thought I only had to pass through the door again, but when I did so on the eve of the full moon—earlier that night I took your satchel—I wasn't given the same strength and

THE DOORWAY

health as a month ago. I felt ..."

He stopped and looked at me.

"It was as if the door ... spoke. It wants me to bring someone else. That's the price of staying young."

It seemed less than likely that a spelled door would grant unending youth in return for merely passing that gift on to another. A rich *pan* might be able to shift the cost of his good life to servants, but someone had to pay in the end. Yaja's last words whispered through my mind, *I paid my own price.*

The smell. Yaja had reeked of it in the days before she died. I'd felt the same urge to run then, too, but at sixteen I thought perhaps it was natural to an old woman dying of some wasting disease. The years since had taught me that no living being should give off such a stench.

Those who'd suspected the plump, pretty girl might not be kin to Yaja were right. For about a month she'd looked after the shop and the herbalist, people said, while Yaja was not seen again until after the girl vanished.

"So once you found yourself unrestored, you came back into town, saw me, and tried to bring me through."

"I'd seen you before, when I came to your shop in the winter to get something for my sick stomach. You gave me herbs and an earful, told me to keep myself cleaner and not drink so much. It struck me afterward that things might have been different if my wife and children hadn't died in the plague, or if I'd taken another wife to look after me. Once I was young again, I thought to come back for you and have another chance."

Wrenched with pity and scorn, I backed away.

"Please," he whimpered but let me go unhindered. Then he

turned and stepped through the door.

*

After a restless night, I arose at the first hint of dawn, checking my stores of herbs and making more of remedies unneeded, just to give my hands something to do. The fingertips that had sunk into the door remained smooth.

Not long after townspeople began setting out for work and errands, someone pounded at the door of my shop. I unbarred it to find Stash. My first thought was of Leshka and the baby, but he said, "They found a sick man outside the north gate this morning. We saw him carried into the gatehouse when we were at the tanner's, and my Jadek sent me to get you."

"I'll go at once."

"Do you want me to come so I can run back if you need anything?"

"No, stay and mind your shop." I locked the door and handed him my ring of keys. "Keep those so Bozhena can get in, if I send someone to fetch herbs or unguents."

When I arrived at the gatehouse, Mirek was standing outside. I walked into the inner room with a guard and found what I had foreseen, a decrepit ruin of a man on a pallet. The leather satchel on the floor told me why the shoemaker had waited. He knew his own work.

I forced myself toward the man through the reek, much worse than it had been the night before. He was thin, with a few strands of white hair clinging to a mottled scalp. The deep blue of his eyes had gone cloudy.

"Do you need anything?" I asked.

"You ..." His voice creaked.

"Yes, it's me."

"I ... hurt."

"Not for long." Yaja had lived barely a week.

Back in the outer room, the guard who'd found him asked, "Can he live?"

I shook my head. "Take him to the hospice." The church would feed and tend him for the days he had left; my herbs were of no use.

"What ails him?"

"Just ... old age."

He held the satchel out. "The shoemaker said this is yours."

It looked a bit dirtier, perhaps, no different otherwise, but its touch repelled me. Mirek said little as we walked back to our street. I told him I still wanted a new satchel, so I left the old one as a pattern when I went to his shop for my keys.

My own shop felt too close. I grew restless, unable to work, and went out. The clear light and sparkling air of a spring morning made me feel a shade less old. As I walked, I wondered whether the east door might somehow draw me back during the next full moon and what would happen to my fingertips if I fought its pull. Would they turn black and die on my hand as I'd seen happen to some with plague or putrid fevers? If so, I'd count it a small price to pay for all that remained.

I paid my own price. Perhaps Yaja had feared growing weak and ill alone, as I did. I wished I'd met her before the door changed her. Had she gone through by ill luck or in search of some path not taken in her youth? In the end, she'd righted the mistake as well as she could, without pulling anyone else into misery, and given me a chance at a life I'd been glad to live.

"Never trust the old," Yaja told me once during the week I'd tended her. "We covet your strength and beauty."

But my Babka hadn't felt that way, and neither did Mirek. Nor did I. I longed to watch Bozhena increase in wisdom, Stash make shoes to take others on journeys, and Leshka's new baby smile and fatten and stumble on the cobblestones until she found her feet.

Streets I'd known for forty years looked new to my eyes. I wandered them as one just arrived in town, until I found myself standing before a door which glowed faintly golden along the top. It was the postern in the west wall, the door of night errands and the dead. As light spread across its thick boards, I knew it was time to seek another to fill my place, one who would learn and thrive as the life within me faded.

The patch of sunlight grew, and with it my knowledge that the moonlit door was barred to me, by Babka's teaching, by Yaja's gift of the shop, by my choice to run from both the manor and unwanted marriage. My path led through the door to the west. I ran my changed hand along its sunlit wood to feel the warmth of a hundred summers.

***

E.L. Mellor attended the Ultimate Science Fiction Workshop in 2008 and the Odyssey Writing Workshop in 2010. When not writing, she works as a freelance academic editor and spends any spare time on music and dance. This is her first published story. Her website can be found, eventually, at elmellor.com.

Serling

Meredith Watts

Betty spotted the cat waiting for them at the front door.

"Watch out!" she cried, but the cat simply stopped licking its paws and looked up at the three people gathered before it.

"Sorry." Betty smiled sheepishly at her husband and their buyer's agent as she scratched the cat behind its ears. "Our cats always try to escape the first chance they get."

"It must like this place," James said as he sipped his iced coffee. "Come on, let's see this oddball house you've fallen in love with."

Betty picked up the little gray tabby cat and cradled him in her arms. "This one's not odd. I swear."

"Ah huh. That's what you said about all the others, too."

"You'll like it."

"I better. We need to find a place to live pronto. Since our landlord's already got a tenant lined up, it's either find a house or find a new apartment."

They followed Carol into the white and black Colonial. A flat screen TV mounted to the wall was quietly playing. Carol crossed the room and shut it off.

Betty gasped as she gazed around the living room. "These hardwood floors—they're gleaming! Oh, and the paint. I just love these colors."

"That's because it's all new," said James. "Everything looks good when it's new."

"You like hardwood floors. You've always said carpeting is just a way to trap dust."

"Oh, I know. It's nice. I'm just trying to stay objective." James peered at one of the windows. "Are these replacement?"

Carol opened the manila folder she'd been carrying with her. "They are. Replaced earlier this year. The floors have been recently redone."

"See?" James said. "New. They're hiding something."

"The owners are very motivated to move this property. They're empty nesters and can't afford to keep it anymore," said Carol. "It's not a short sale, but I think it's very nearly one. This economy has forced a lot of people to sell."

Betty held the cat in one arm while she ran her fingers over the intricate trim on the mantle. "This wood work is wonderful. It reminds me of all the work your dad did at your parents' place."

James nodded. "I like how it's stained and not painted. Looks more natural."

Betty winked. "I told you that you'd like this place."

"We've already fallen in love with a dozen different houses and had them slip through our fingers. I'm not ready to commit and watch you get heartbroken again just yet."

Carol said, "I'd like you both to take good mental notes as we go through the property. The selling agent was adamant that we give him feedback. Apparently no one does."

"No one?" Betty asked as she stroked the cat's soft fur. It closed its eyes and purred.

"Not a soul. They sign in, and he never hears from them again."

James grunted. "There must be something wrong with it."

Betty smiled, absently stroking the purring cat. "Maybe we'll find out as we look through the house."

"Maybe."

James glanced out the picture window. The house sat on its own little hill above its neighbors. The rusty, weathered "For Sale" sign waved at passersby with a practiced sway.

"I think this house looks regal," Betty said as she stood next to her husband.

"Castles look regal, not houses."

"I'm just saying it looks nice. Lovely green lawn. Beautiful landscaping. It even has a fountain."

"Water features are mosquito breeding grounds."

"You're just trying to convince yourself you don't want the place. Give in. This could be the one."

James glanced back at Carol. "How long has it been on the market?"

Carol flipped through the listing. "Four hundred, thirty-nine days, and it's had twelve price changes."

"Geez. Betty, what is it with you and these houses that just languish?"

"I dunno. I feel sorry for them, I suppose. And people have forgotten about them, so there's less of a chance we'll have to compete with someone else to get it."

"Competition is healthy," James said.

"For the seller's wallet. I don't like feeling rushed. I like the idea that we can take our time."

"Of course, dear." James kissed his wife's cheek. "There are probably bodies in the basement. Should we find out now or later?"

"I want to see the living areas first." Betty cooed at the cat as she fiddled with its name tag. "Because living things are far more fun than dead things. Aren't they, Serling?"

Serling purred and flicked his tail.

*

"Here's the kitchen," Carol said. "White ceramic tile floor is new. The appliances are all energy efficient and come with the property."

"Stainless steel," James said with a glance at his wife. "Nice. I think if we put a matching bottle opener on this granite counter top, or if we got rid of the refrigerator and put in a beer dispensary ... I could really love those maple cabinets if I could mount a tap—"

Betty laughed. "Oh, I don't think so."

"Are you sure? Because even though I know you've always wanted a stove with sealed burners, I was sort of envisioning an indoor grill."

"Yeah, I can see that too." She rubbed the cat's belly. "Can't you, Serling? An indoor grill, a charming outdoor husband, and his lovely indoor Inger Stevens wife who spends quality time with the milkman."

Serling purred.

"We can't be having that," James said. He put one hand on his wife's shoulder.

Serling meowed loudly and flicked his tail.

James sipped his coffee and half-choked.

Betty frowned. "Are you okay?"

"Yeah, I just got a mouthful of cream."

"If there weren't coffee in it, I'd say give it to Serling. You'd like that wouldn't you, Serling? Some nice cream?"

He shook his coffee and drank a sip. "All better. And all for me. None for the kitty."

The cat hissed.

"Someone's got a temper." James slurped more. His face contorted and he ran to the sink and spat out the coffee. "Whatever they put in this was rancid."

Betty grinned. "That's what you get for taunting the cat."

James turned on the tap and drank a swallow to rinse his mouth out. He held up his drink. "Carol, is it okay if I throw this away here?"

She nodded. "If you want, there's a half bath just over there. Make sure you clean up after yourself."

"A half bath?" Betty asked as her husband disappeared behind the door. "That's nice. Right near the living room. Perfect for guests."

"Exactly. It has new fixtures. Chrome."

Betty peeked over Carol's shoulder at the packet of pictures. "Shiny. And so modern. Can we keep this printout?"

"Absolutely."

James emerged from the bathroom, wiping his mouth on the back of his hand.

Carol smiled. "On to the dining room?"

*

Betty gazed up at the brilliant arrangement of light and crystal. "The chandelier comes with the place, right?"

"Light fixtures can't be excluded," James said.

Carol shook her head. "They can, but they aren't in this place."

Betty batted at one of the crystals. Serling's paw followed the dancing light as it waltzed across Betty's sweater. His tail flicked mischievously. "Look at the pattern it makes on the wall!"

"The buyers even list the furniture as negotiable," said Carol.

Betty's eyes lit up. "You mean we could have this dining room table?"

Carol nodded.

"And the leather sofa in the living room?" James asked.

Carol frowned. "Sorry, I missed it before. They exclude the leather sofa."

Serling meowed happily and played with Betty's sleeve.

James scowled. "You should really put that cat down. You're getting covered in hair, and you don't know where it's been. It's going to ruin your sweater."

Serling fussed in Betty's arms.

"See? Even the cat wants down."

Betty sighed. "Fine."

She put Serling on the refinished white oak floor. The cat danced around Betty's legs, butting his head against Betty's calf, all the while staring up at James with his dark orange eyes and flicking his tail.

Carol looked at the couple. "Onward and upward?"

*

James and Betty stood and stared at the staircase leading upstairs.

"Okay, I'm starting to understand why this house is still here," James said.

Betty nodded, eyes wide. "Carol, you can tell the seller's agent that this is weird."

Carol flipped through the pictures. "I don't understand. This must be new. It's not what the pictures show."

James pointed at the carpet covering the stairs, the wall and ceiling. "This isn't new. Look at it. There are stains. The cat has been shredding it for months. And it smells like litter. I thought you said the sellers were motivated."

As if on cue Serling climbed halfway up the wall, his tail twitching with the joy of the hunt. He bit at the beige carpet loops and pulled as though he were a cheetah trying to conquer an antelope.

"I'll be sure to tell the sellers." Carol brightened. "Though, it is just cosmetic. It shouldn't be harder to remove than wallpaper."

James grunted. "I don't suppose we can get a concession for bad taste?"

"The bedrooms are better," Carol promised. "The master bedroom has nearly three hundred square feet, two closets, and a full bath with marble tile and all new fixtures. There's a skylight and —"

James and Betty froze in the doorway.

"And scratch-post for carpeting," James said.

Carol frowned. "No, this is supposed to be hardwood. Refinished pine with a pumpkin tint. I don't understand."

Betty walked across the patches of clawed corrugated cardboard and mangled carpet. "Cat people are crazy."

James followed. "But there's only one cat."

"That we've seen. I'm not sure I want to go in the basement. No dead human bodies, but maybe a cemetery for the thirty cats that came before this one. Or maybe the rest of the herd is down there, waiting for us to walk into their trap." Betty winced. "At a minimum, I bet the basement smells like cat pee."

Serling rolled around at Betty's feet. Betty squatted and rubbed his light gray belly. Serling flicked his tail back and forth blissfully.

"That smell will go away," James said.

Betty shook her head. "It won't. There are certain smells that just leech into everything and never leave."

James knelt beside Betty and petted the cat. "We should give it a chance."

"Really? You've fallen in love with the place now? After everything you've just seen?" Betty frowned. "Carol, I think we're done here."

Carol nodded. "You two aren't cat people, then?"

Betty laughed. "Not this much. We do have cats now, but I have to say I'm more of a dog person."

Serling clawed Betty's hand. Betty shrieked and recoiled.

"That's what you get for preferring dogs," James said.

Serling leaped to his feet, arched his back and hissed.

"What's wrong, kitty?" James asked.

Betty shook her head. "He's as crazy as his owners."

Serling spat and ran from the room.

"Come back here!" James climbed to his feet and raced after the strange gray tabby.

"James! Where are you going? Don't chase the cat!" Betty followed him down the carpeted stairs into the living room, but everything had changed. She spun around in one direction, then in the other, trying to take it all in. "James, where are you? This is weird."

The walls were wallpapered; the floor, carpeted; the furniture, covered in plastic. A black and white console TV was the central focus of the living room. Some 1960s show chirped in the background.

James raced into the room. "Betty, what are you wearing?"

Betty stared down at herself. She was dressed in a yellow and blue plaid dress with cowgirl boots. She looked up at her husband. "What are you wearing?"

James saw himself in the mirror over the fireplace. "Jesus Christ, I got dressed by 'Leave It to Beaver.'"

"This isn't right. What's going on?"

He shook his head. "I don't know. Carol! Where are you?"

Serling appeared in the doorway to the kitchen, flicking his tail. Betty started crossing the room to the tabby, until she saw it was playing with a mouse. She flinched and turned away.

"Oh, James. The cat's got a mouse!"

James grabbed Betty's shoulders. "Can you believe it, Betty?"

"Believe what?"

"This house! It's a steal, Betty. I tell you: A steal!"

Betty shook her head. "No, it's not. There's something very wrong here. We need to leave. Right now."

Serling rubbed himself against Betty's leg, purring, looking up at her with dark orange eyes, a dead mouse hanging from his jaws.

Betty backed away. James caught her, wrapped his arms around her. "There, there, Betty. Your cat brought us a present to celebrate our new home. If he keeps this up, I might start to like him."

She pushed her husband away. "James, that's not my cat. This isn't our home. Why are you acting this way? Why did everything go retro?"

James looked down at the cat and frowned. "Oh, no. The children will be upset."

Betty shook her head. "We don't have children."

James pointed at the dead mouse. "I told you a pet mouse was a bad idea with a cat in the house, and now we'll have to tell the children that Carol is dead."

"Carol? Are you saying that mouse is Carol? And she's dead?"

James put his arm across her shoulders. "It's just a mouse, honey. Let's not make a big deal out of it."

"But Carol was our Buyer's Agent!"

"What are you talking about?"

Betty shook her head. Her heart was beating so hard it threatened to choke her. James swatted her on the backside. "Now get into the kitchen and make me a martini."

"You don't drink martinis."

James threw himself on the plastic-covered couch. "You've always liked making me martinis."

Betty shook her head, backing away from him. It was all she could do to keep from screaming or falling into a scared and shivering puddle. None of this was right or made sense or anything. She needed air. She needed her husband.

She needed to leave.

She bumped against the front door, spun, and scrabbled at the knob. It wouldn't open.

She ran through the dining room. The chandelier she'd loved was gone, replaced by something bronze and hideous. Teal wallpaper covered the walls. The floor had linoleum where beautiful hardwood once gleamed. Betty ran into the kitchen and threw herself against the back door.

"Please, let me out!" she sobbed, beating her fists against the unmoving door. "Someone help us!"

Serling rubbed up against her leg. Betty screamed and kicked the cat away. The cat glared up at her.

A timer dinged.

"Is that what I think it is?" James shouted from the living room.

Betty looked away from the cat. "What do you think it is?"

"Your famous tuna casserole, of course!"

The cat sat before her, tail covering its feet like a blanket. Betty inched around him, keeping as far away as possible. The stainless steel stove she'd admired was nowhere to be seen. Betty opened the white enameled oven door and looked in.

Tuna casserole.

Serling rubbed against her leg and purred. Betty slammed the stove shut with a bang. "Just get away from me!"

Serling hissed and ran from the room.

Betty ran her hands through her 1950s perm. What was she supposed to do now?

"Is it done yet, honey? I'm starving."

"James, we have to get out of here."

"But you worked all day to make that casserole."

"It's burned. I burned it. We should go out. How do you feel about going out?"

Silence.

"James, I'll make you that martini, okay?" What was in a martini? Betty didn't know. James only drank beer. "Then we'll go out to eat."

Still nothing.

"James? Where are you?"

Betty ran from the kitchen into the living room. James wasn't there. She ran upstairs. The stairwell was a lovely shade of blue;

the carpet that had covered it all was gone. She looked in the master bedroom and saw everything Carol had promised: spacious with gleaming hardwood. No strange cat features.

But James wasn't there.

She looked into the other bedrooms, into the bathrooms, into the closets, and still no James.

"James? We can eat the casserole if you'd like," she called as she came down the stairs. More hardwood. Normal colors. Leather sofa. It was as though the flash to the past had never happened. The sellers would return soon. Their time here was coming to an end. "Let's go out. I want a walk."

The cat was waiting for her in the middle of the living room. A small mouse wriggled in its paws.

Betty's heart thundered. Her eyes went wide. "Oh, God. James? Let him go. You let him go right—"

The cat bit down. Blood dripped onto its paws. Its glowing eyes never left Betty's.

Betty sank to the floor. Tears streamed down her face.

"What do you want?" she cried.

The cat poked at the broken body of the mouse, seemed disappointed that it wasn't moving, and looked back up at Betty.

"Please, just let me go. We just wanted to buy a house! Why are you doing this?"

Betty heard a rattling of keys at the front door. A sob of relief burst from her. She'd get out. She'd be safe. Betty scrambled to her feet, lunging for the door as it opened.

But just as she found herself looking up at the blinding light of the sun, tears streaming down her face, relieved that she was free, darkness shrouded her. Pain pricked her sides like sharp spears. A woman's screams filled her ears.

Betty curled in on herself, shivering and whimpering in the warm shadows.

"What is it?" she heard a man say.

Where were these people? Why could she hear them, but not see them? Betty did her best to call for help, but all that came out of her were feeble squeaks.

"Look!" the woman shrieked. "Look at what the cat did!"

The man groaned in disgust. "Two dead mice? Serling outdid himself. Did you leave these trespassers as gifts for us or for the buyers?"

"Just get rid of them."

"Come on, Serling. Scoot. Your prizes are mine now."

Light shone in on her. Betty found herself looking up into the face of a man she didn't recognize, but she didn't care. She reached out for him, calling for him, warning him, urging him to get away. The man poked her with an impossibly massive finger.

"Three mice. And this one's still kicking."

Mice? No. She wasn't a mouse. She was a woman and needed to get out of here, needed a hospital. Didn't they understand?

"I told you we have a pest problem. No wonder no one buys this place when these vermin keep showing up."

"Serling just doesn't want to leave. He hates all these people coming and going."

"Mark, what are you doing? Don't play with it. You're as bad as the cat. I swear if we let Serling have his way, he'd play dress up with the things he kills."

The man chuckled. "Maybe we shouldn't leave the TV on for him. It gives him ideas."

"Just kill it and be done."

"You heard her, Serling. Kill the nasty rodent. Make it quick."

Betty shuddered. Cold fear chilled her to the bone. Her breath froze in her lungs as dark orange eyes filled her vision. A huge maw opened filled with columns of fangs.

*

Serling stretched and yawned before settling himself by the front door, tail twitching slowly.

***

Meredith Watts spends her days as an unassuming instructor of mathematics, and her nights trying to get as far away from calculus and fractions as possible. She currently has a contract with Masque Books to publish her full-length novel Heart of the Matter, *a crime drama set in a world of zombies told from the perspective of a woman who counsels the undead as they transition into unlife. Meredith can be found at https://theplatypusconnection.wordpress.com/ where she pursues her other loves of platypodes and gluten-free cooking, when she remembers to say anything at all.*

Part II:
Perception and Transformation

The Test

Talib S. Hussain

Trixie had been shouting outside the door for over a minute when I finally decided to activate my main sensors. "Hurry up, Charlene. We're going to be late for class!" she yelled.

"Yeah, yeah," I shouted, fully online at last. "Give me a few millis." Trixie is the best friend a young bot could ever hope to have, but she was always a bit radical about being on time.

I grabbed my memory augmentation chip. We had System Analysis today—taught by the totally boring Professor Wesley. Our plan was to show up, set our visuals and aurals to full-spectrum record, and then tune out to play a game of Surreal. We were currently our dormitory champions and had our circuits set on beating the top-ranked campus pair—only two levels ahead of us. That meant play, play, play.

I inserted the chip into my auxiliary memory slot. A few millis later, it verified and I was ready to go. My cubicle door opened automatically as soon as I got near it.

Trixie stood waiting outside, tapping her foot in a very human gesture of impatience. She was programmed that way. Tall, slender, and with very human-form bodies and rich facial expressions, the TX750s were intended primarily to serve as personal assistants in human-run businesses. By contrast, my CH340 model line was designed for all-terrain communication infrastructure development and maintenance. We're squat, powerful, treaded and hardened—uggh! A cube with wheels is better looking than I am.

"Hey Trix, what's new?" I asked, as my cubicle door closed and locked itself behind me.

"Hey yourself," she replied, "Not much new, but I did catch some bytes that Test Day will be announced soon." Her facials were normal, but I could detect subtle fluctuations in her voice patterns.

"What's up?" I asked. "You worried?"

Trixie looked around at the other bots in the hallway and didn't reply right away. Never give away free bytes to in-range sensors, as they say. After all, who knew what would give you the edge over the other bots on the Test. "Naw, Charlie. I'm not worried, just excited," she finally said. "Let's get outside where the air is clear." That was our code for a private chat.

I winked one of my antennae in understanding and led the way down the ramp to the dormitory exit. Don't get me started on my antennae. Really, no other models have external antennae anymore—the internal ones have been proven to be just as effective. But, that's the CH340 designers for you—old school all the way.

A couple of minutes later, we were heading to the Bot Mind Development Center at our usual pace. Trixie with her long legs walked slowly beside me as I rolled along as quickly as I could. I may be slow now, but Trix and most other bots won't be able to hold a laser to me once I graduate and get my full citizen upgrade.

We went our favorite way, along the indirect route that passed the statue of the founding father of all bots, Dr. Turing. There were rarely any other bots on this path, but we loved it and often used this time to chat privately. Of course, there were always Landscaping Wipes around keeping the campus grounds in order, but it's not like they could steal bytes given their rigid, limited programming.

"I'm not worried for myself, but for Jason," Trixie said.

"Jason—what a waste!" I replied. "You're a top of the line TX750, and he's a lowly JS210 construction bot. Why did you ever choose him for a life partner?"

"You're just jealous," Trix said, "No one's been asking you to share bytes."

She was right of course. I was as jealous as my emotion circuits would let me get—but not for that reason. Trix and I had been assigned as student partners the day we were both activated, and had spent over 80% of our non-rest time together ever since. Until Jason came into the picture, we had shared almost every byte of information we'd ever learned with each other. I hated that Jason took precious time from us. After all, once we passed the Test, I'd probably never see Trixie again.

I waited a minute for my emotion circuits to reset to baseline before replying. Trixie, a bit heated herself, kept quiet too.

"Okay, so you're worried about Jason," I said, "but why? He's fully functional and therefore almost certain to pass the Test."

"He's near the bottom of the rankings."

"The Surreal rankings? What does that have to do with the Test?"

Despite the best efforts of our generation of student bots at predicting what skills the Test was looking for, none of us knew anything definitive except that dysfunctional bots inevitably failed and we were pretty sure that better Test scores led to better job assignments. It was near impossible to analyze though, since no bot that passed would ever talk about it, and the bots that failed were Wiped and could no longer engage in conversation at all.

"Well, I heard some bytes in the library this morning while you were resting," Trixie replied. "A couple of IR50's were speculating that the Test might be based on Surreal."

"You listened to data analysis bots? You know they generate hundreds of speculations every day. It's not worth wasting the memory on their bytes."

"I know, I know," Trixie replied. "But, remember last year? Another JS210 failed and he was pretty low in the Surreal rankings, too. Maybe there's something wrong with Jason's line."

"Trix, that was just an outlier," I said. "That JS210 may have failed, but another 647 passed last year."

"I suppose," she said, looking down.

Oh well, what can we do? Our designers program us to care about the bots we're close to. No way around that. I hadn't found a life partner yet, but if what Trix felt for Jason was anything like what I felt for her, of course she'd worry.

We reached the statue, and as usual stopped for a moment to reflect. It was very inspiring to see the human who had created the science of computers that hundreds of years later led to us. He had also given us the Test that allowed us citizenship.

"What a great man," Trix said, sighing. "I hope my human is just as great."

Trixie said pretty much the same thing every time—she's nothing if not consistent. I gave my usual response, "I'm sure he or she will be, especially with you helping as a full citizen."

Being a full citizen was supposed to be awesome. From watching the training videos, we could see how much more fun life was as a citizen. Citizen bots had bodies with all their physical capabilities enabled, got to interact with humans, were actually able to manipulate objects in the real world that weren't just part of their bodies, and didn't have to worry about learning new stuff all the time.

"I can't wait to move objects. After all our fun interacting virtually in Surreal, I'm sure the real thing will be super fun too."

"Yeah—it sure will," Trix said.

"Hey, if you want, I'll spend some time teaching Jason to play Surreal better to see if we can bump up his rankings."

"Really? That would be awesome! You're so good at explaining things. Thanks Charlene!" Trixie glowed as she said this. And I do mean glowed. Humans like to know when their assistants are feeling happy, so Trix actually had a luminescent layer under her facial features, one that was currently a nice soft shade of yellow. Me, I just had a small, red light-emitting diode on my undercarriage that activated when I was low on battery. If I could sigh, I would.

We were quiet the rest of the way to the Center. As programmed, we paused for a moment before entering to reflect on campus motto—'Learn What You Can'—carved in large letters over the entrance. I had certainly learned something new about myself. Helping Jason! I must be crazy.

*

"Now, turn to the left and place your hand on the security scanner before opening that door," I said using the Surreal voice comms.

"Scanner? What scanner?" Jason asked. "There's nothing here except for a plain brown door."

"I told you to make your game character put on its augmented reality lenses, you dunce," I comm'd. "This game level is about maintaining physical and cyber security. You need to follow all the rules to verify the system and identify any threats. And, if you violate security yourself, you will be identified as a threat."

After three hours of playing Surreal, he was still making the most basic errors–and we were only playing level eight. "What the heck was Trix thinking?" I muttered to myself.

Jason, engrossed in losing his game to the best of his ability, ignored my directions as usual and opened the virtual door. A couple of hundred millis later, it was all over. Again.

"Enough. We're done," I said as I ended the session and pulled my game chip out of its slot. The game world faded as my sensors quickly focused on the wall of the recreational cubicle we were sitting in.

"Ouch! Why'd you do that?" Jason asked as he pulled his own chip and slowly adjusted back to seeing the real world. Not everyone can tune in and out as easily as I can, I'm proud to say.

"Shut up, you idiot. You're a construction bot. You don't even have pain sensors."

Jason started mumbling something about trying harder, but I ignored him. "I've got to go," I said. Without another glance at him, I left the recreational cubicle and headed to my resting cubicle on the floor below. Thinking about Jason, a clear example of failure in decision-making skills, made me wonder about life partners once again.

Humans wanted intelligent servants and friendly companions,

not mindless slaves, and thus they had designed us to require social interaction at the most fundamental levels. Any bot left alone
for too long would suffer irreparable damage to its emotion circuits and become dysfunctional. Hence, we were assigned a student partner immediately after assembly, and could either choose
or be assigned a life partner to share our lives with as full citizens.

Most student partners stayed together as life partners. But, I
was destined to roam far and wide repairing communication infrastructure, while Trixie would always be based near her human
in a city. Jason could be assigned to construction jobs within the
same city and stay near her all the time. I hadn't found a match
yet, and would likely have to be assigned one. Who would it be?
Would I like him or her? Would he or she be as awesome as Trix?

A couple of minutes later I was plugged into my charger staring
at the back wall of my resting cubicle. I had three hours before I
had to be at my next class—Human Interaction—and needed
every second of rest I could get to recover from my frustrating experience with Jason.

*

Trixie was shouting outside my door as usual when I activated my
sensors. "Hurry up, Charlene. Class is about to start!"

"Yeah, yeah," I shouted, as I slowly took in my cubicle's surroundings. I checked my internal clock. As usual, we had plenty
of time.

Half an hour later, as we sat together in the second row of the
Human Interaction class, Trix gushed quietly, "He's so awesome!"

"You just have a crush on Professor Brandon." It was hardly a
challenge teasing Trixie. Of course, as expected, she blushed.

That luminescence layer could certainly glow a nice shade of red.

Professor Brandon was a dynamic presenter for a human. Over the past few weeks, he had introduced us to the theory of human-bot interaction and had led us through enactments of eight of the top ten interactions most of us would encounter. So far, we'd covered giving and receiving directions, handling criticism and praise, exchanging negative and positive emotions, collaborating, and entertaining. The Professor had emphasized how each interaction needed to be looked at from two sides—the human side and the bot side—and how every interaction could flow from human to bot and from bot to human. It was really challenging, and I appreciated the symmetry of the theory. My favorite interaction had been in positive emotion exchange. The professor had enacted an "I love you bot" interaction and used Jason as the target. It had been hilarious to see Jason stammering nervously as he had tried to figure out how and whether to reciprocate. I had full-spectrum recorded that entire session and had played it back to myself several times since.

"Now, the ninth top machine-human interaction is one of the hardest," Professor Brandon was saying. "Trust."

He pointed dramatically at a GR73 farming bot sitting in the front row. "You, Grace," he asked, "did you do your homework from the last class?" He had asked us to find another human on campus and do something to entertain them.

"Yes, sir," Grace replied happily.

"Well, I don't trust you—bots can't ever be trusted," he said.

We were all shocked. Trixie and I looked at each other. What did that mean? Everyone knew bots were programmed to never lie. Of course we could be trusted.

"I'm sorry, sir," Grace stammered in a good application of what to do when receiving criticism.

"Not good enough. You'll have to prove it to me. "

"I can't," she said, "I didn't record it—I was too excited."

My emotion circuits buzzed a little. I really liked Grace and hated to see her upset. "Professor," I called out, "You asked Grace a question and she answered. Bots can't lie. Grace is a bot, therefore she didn't lie. She must have done her homework." I was quite proud of myself for making the conclusion.

Professor Brandon completely ignored me, and loomed over Grace. After a full minute, with Grace frozen into immobility due to his closeness—and the rest of us frozen too in sympathetic reaction—he stepped back and addressed the whole class. "Always remember," he said, "just because bots are programmed not to lie, doesn't mean that humans will believe you. Always record evidence of what you've done. Full-spectrum recordings are fool-proof and even admissible in a court of law."

I made a little sound to catch his attention.

"Yes, Charlene," he asked.

"Sir, what's the other side of this interaction?" I asked.

"Good question. When can a bot trust a human?"

Trixie shot up her hand and eagerly called out, "That's easy. We can always trust humans. They programmed us, after all."

"Interesting," he said and paused to stare at each of us. "That leads us to our final human-bot interaction," he continued. "Fear. What do you do when a human is scared of you?"

He walked slowly around the room, looking intently at each bot in turn. Two rows up from me, he stopped and pointed at another GR73. "I think you're smarter than me, Grant, and that scares me."

"Oh no, Sir, you're much smarter than me," Grant said.

"Prove it!" he commanded. "Prove you're not as smart as me. Now!"

Grant remained silent, unsure of what to do. Seconds turned into several minutes before the Professor gave him a hint. "Can you do calculus, Grant?"

Grant flashed his big eyes and happily said "No, sir, I can't."

Professor Brandon nodded his head. "Well, that's great. I can, so I must be smarter."

That made a great deal of sense to me, and I could see most of the other bots nodding, winking, or verbally agreeing.

"Of course," he said after a little pause, "that's only if I decide to trust you are telling the truth."

Wow, these last two interactions were tough. How could we interact properly with a human who didn't trust us and feared us?

He started walking around the class again. Finally, he stopped in front of me.

"So, Charlene, I have a very real worry about Grant," he said. "What would you do if you were in my shoes?"

Imagining shoes on my treads made my emotion circuits hum with humor. But, after a few millis, I thought more seriously about his question. "Sir," I said, "I would apply the 2-step system analysis procedure we were taught in System Analysis class. If he checks out as functional and uncompromised, that would prove he's trustworthy and doesn't need to be feared."

The Professor said nothing to me in reply, and instead just turned and walked back to the front of the class. "Your homework is to figure out what Charlene missed—if she missed something. Class dismissed."

*

Later that evening, Trix and I went to the campus library to study. While we could have just let our systems process our daily lessons during our rest cycle, we preferred to learn the old-fashioned human way—by goofing off as we pretended to review our work. Of course, there was another perk—sometimes in the library you could overhear some bytes that might come in handy later. Evening was always a busy time, with probably half the bots on campus crammed into rows and rows of study carrels.

Trixie and I were seated together facing each other in our favorite carrel right in the middle of the library. To a casual sensor, we seemed to be watching a video summary of the lessons of the day on the two-sided screen in between us. However, we actually had our game chips slotted in and were playing Surreal—and kicking some metal ass.

We had flown through three game levels in record time and had reached level 57—only one level behind the campus leader now. This level had an asteroid belt mining setting and was based on a real-life incident from the last century when mining bots had first been deployed. Pirates had reprogrammed over thirty bots to send their ore to them instead of to the bots' owners before the authorities had caught on.

I was playing the pilot of a patrol ship and Trixie was playing the sensor officer. Our goal was to find as many of the mining bots as possible and determine if they had been compromised, all without revealing ourselves to or getting caught by the simulated pirates. I loved my role. Being able to control the movement of a ship, even a virtual one, felt powerful, and I was really good at keeping one or more asteroids between our ship and the closest pirate. We had been playing the level for almost an hour and had found and investigated over twenty-five bots. Of those, nine had programming that differed from factory specs.

One thing that kept Surreal interesting was how much more detailed the levels got as you moved higher. In this level, our characters were so much like our real selves that my emotion circuits zinged a little every time I had my character look at Trixie's character.

"Hey—ship sensors indicate multiple bots on that huge asteroid on our port side," Trixie comm'd. "Let's check it out."

We both liked the voice communications since we could talk via our game chips and not worry about being overheard.

"Turning to port now," I replied. "There is some dust in the way, so I need to focus. Keep your sensors on that pirate—he's right on the other side of that big rock. If he starts to poke his nose out, let me know."

A few millis later, we landed safely on the asteroid in a small crater and sent out our probes. It didn't take long before they returned with amazing results—there were 43 mining bots on the asteroid, all clustered in a single large cavern. My emotion chip surged. This could nail us the level! Trix and I quickly put on our virtual space debris protection suits and exited the ship in our virtual rover.

"This is so awesome," I comm'd as I zoomed the rover around the barren asteroid-scape.

"It sure is," Trixie replied. "Hey, what do you think it'll be like when we're full citizens? Do you think things will be exciting like this or just boring?"

"Trix," I replied, "life will never be boring for you. You'll become the life of the party. Think of it, not only will you be able to dance with your human and make him or her look good, you'll also be able to help with your human's social and business events, make beautiful decorations, and arrange the office furniture into interesting patterns whenever you want just to keep things fresh and new."

"Yeah, that would be cool," she comm'd, "I just hope I don't make mistakes. Remember that older TX we saw last week in the training video about the dangers of Cause and Effect?"

Did I remember? That may have been the scariest video they had shown us in our entire time on campus. A female TX620 that must have been assembled at least two centuries ago was the only bot in the video. For almost the entire video, all she had done was wave at people arriving for her human's evening party, greet them with a cheery "Hello Sir" or "Hello Ma'am", and open the front door of the house for them. But when the last guest had arrived, she had not paid careful enough attention and had hit the human in the head with the door as she opened it. The poor man had bled from a cut on his forehead. I, and every other bot in class, had been so shocked we had all immediately gone into shutdown. When the instructor had reactivated us, thankfully facing a blank video screen, he had only needed to say the point of the lesson once for us all to get it—once we were citizens and could manipu-late objects, we could easily be a danger to humans if we weren't vigilant at all times.

"Stop worrying Trixie," I joked. "You're thirteen generations more advanced than she was. You could never be more than half as silly as she was."

"Awww, Charlene," Trix replied back, "that's so sweet. That may be true, but at least I can always count on one thing—I'll never be as silly as you."

To underscore her point, I made the rover do a little spin-out. Trixie let go a peal of laughter over the comms—I always love hearing her voice simulator engage, but when she laughs, it really makes my emotion circuits sizzle. We drove the rest of the way to the bot encampment in happy silence.

*

An hour later, after interviewing and examining 34 of the mining bots, I was no longer happy. We were running out of time to finish the level and hadn't made any real progress. When we had arrived, we had found all 43 bots activated but standing immobile along the wall from one side of the cavern to the other. It was strange—all the other mining bots we had investigated had been actively mining when we found them. Since they were so conveniently lined up though, we had simply started at one end of the line and begun analyzing them one by one.

All of the bots so far had checked out, so this was looking like a dead-end. I wanted to cut loose and try to find a better asteroid, but every time I tried to convince Trixie we should leave, she repeated the same thing: "No way, Charlie! We're doing them all, and that's that!" That's my Trix, once she gets something into her circuits, she won't let it go.

With the 35th bot, Trixie started the analysis as usual with the standard set of ten questions we had been taught in System Analysis class.

"Are you operating within normal parameters?" she asked using the in-game character voice chat.

"Yes," the bot replied.

"Has your programming been altered by a non-authorized source?"

"No"

"Have you logged any system warnings or errors since activation?"

"No"

"Have you had any unexpected physical contact with another bot or with a human?"

"No"

The remaining six questions were further queries about the status of key physical and logical circuits. As with all the previous bots, the current one reported no issues to all questions.

To finish our analysis, I took charge of the next step—passing a simulated circuit analyzer tool slowly over the entire bot. The readout on the analyzer remained a steady green throughout.

"This one is clean too," I comm'd to Trixie, "35 down, 8 to go." I checked the game clock. "And we only have 15 minutes left."

"Almost there," Trixie replied eagerly, as she moved on to number 36.

She was six questions in when I suddenly had a realization. "Hey ... this reminds me of Professor Brandon's homework today. How do we know they are telling us the truth?"

"Silly Charlie," Trixie replied, "you know bots can't lie. And anyway, the homework was about the human-bot interaction of fear. We're not humans, so why would we fear another bot?"

"Yeah, I know," I said. "But, what if they are actually lying to us? What if they are a danger to us? How could we tell? And, these are simulated bots, after all, not real ones."

"That shouldn't matter," Trixie said after a little pause to reflect. "The Surreal game is designed to challenge us on what can happen in the real world, not some make-believe one. So, the same rules must apply as in the real world."

My logic circuits couldn't find a flaw in her reasoning but my emotion circuits were signaling dissatisfaction. I thought about it for a few more millis and then gave up.

"Okay, I suppose that must be right," I said, finally. "Let's just hurry up and get this over with."

We just managed to finish with the last bot before we ran out of time. All of them had been uncompromised. Our level summary said "Level Failed: Insufficient Threats Found". I checked the leader-board—the lead pair had passed their level and were again two ahead of us.

"I'm done for the night," I comm'd, my emotion circuits running hot. "See you out there." Without waiting for a reply, I pulled my game chip.

My sensors tuned in quickly to the library around us. It was less than a quarter full now, and several Cleaning Wipes had started polishing the floors. I waited a couple of minutes while Trixie disconnected and re-adjusted to normal reality. In silence we headed out of the library and back to the dorm.

"Awww, Charlene," Trixie said as we reached my resting cubicle, "don't be upset. I know you hate to lose. But, we're still close."

"Yeah, yeah," I mumbled, "see you tomorrow." I entered my cubicle and let the door shut behind me, cutting off Trixie's soft "Good night."

*

"Hurry up, Charlene," Trixie yelled from outside my door, "they just posted the news. It's Test Day!"

"Coming!" I yelled back. Test Day! I was so excited that I slapped in my memory augmentation chip and rushed out of my cubicle before it had even finished verifying.

"Hey Charlene isn't this awesome? By the end of the day we'll be full citizens!"

"Yeah, the first thing I'm going to do is give someone a high-five!"

Hundreds of bot pairs were lined up as we approached the Test Facility. We moved forward slowly but steadily, and ten minutes later reached the main entrance. Above the doors was the graduation motto "Do What You've Learned." Now, it may be a subtle distinction from the campus motto, but I've always liked the symmetry.

We entered and checked the large overhead assignment board for our test location. "Oh great!" Trixie cried. "We're taking the test in neighboring cubicles. That means we can be together right until the end."

I winked one of my antennae in agreement. We'd heard bytes that student pairs tested together, but it was nice to have it confirmed.

We headed to our cubicles, and stood quietly in front of them. The line of bots on either side of us seemed to stretch forever. We had been standing quietly for almost an hour when a loud chime sounded throughout the building and all the doors opened at the same time. Trix gave me a quick wave as we both entered our cubicles. The doors shut automatically behind us.

The cubicle was empty. A single phrase appeared on the screen on the wall. "Activate game chip."

Game chip? That seemed a bit odd, but I got out my chip and slotted it in. A few millis later, my chip verified. Immediately, I found myself in a familiar game world. I was on board the bridge of a simulated ship looking out into space. It looked just like the mining scenario from Surreal!

"Hey pilot, let's get a move on!" a familiar voice said over the out-of-band comms.

"Trixie!" I yelled. I turned my character around and sure enough, Trix's character was at her station dressed as the sensor officer. "This is so weird."

"Yeah, I know," Trixie responded. "It looks like the Test is going to be a game of Surreal. I wonder how that is even possible."

"I don't know. But, let's keep our eyes open. Maybe the rules will be different," I said.

*

Almost an hour later, it seemed clear that the Test was exactly the same as the Surreal scenario we had just played the night before. We had found the same twenty-five bots in the same locations, and the same nine had been compromised.

"Hey Charlene," Trixie comm'd, "sensors indicate multiple bots again on the same asteroid as last night."

"Let's search somewhere else," I suggested, "we need to pass the Test and that's probably a dead-end."

"Yeah, I agree."

We headed away from the large asteroid towards the one quadrant of the belt we hadn't explored already. Forty minutes later, we had found—and avoided—several pirate ships, but hadn't found any other bots.

"Let's get back to that large asteroid," Trixie comm'd. "We're going to run out of time. Maybe some of them will be different now."

"Yeah—this isn't working out"

I quickly flew the ship to the large asteroid, keeping out of sight of the pirates, and landed in the same crater as before. Since we had a good idea of where the bots were, Trix and I decided to just suit up our characters and head straight there to save time. Unlike before, I didn't really enjoy driving the rover. My emotion circuits were a little spiky—I guess I was getting nervous.

We arrived at the same cavern with only 30 minutes left to play. The same 43 bots were there, lined up as before, and we quickly started analyzing them—two at a time. Trix would ask questions of one bot while I scanned another, and then we'd swap.

We analyzed all the bots in record time—only 20 minutes— but found no threats. After bot 43, my emotion circuits hit their limit. I stopped and wheeled out of the cavern. After a few millis, Trix followed after me.

"What is going on?" I comm'd. "There were no other bots to find and it's looking like none of these are compromised. How are we going to pass? We know at least one other bot pair passed this level. Did we miss another asteroid somehow?"

"We scanned almost the entire belt. There's got to be an answer here somewhere. Do you think these bots could be lying to us?" Trixie asked.

"We went over this last time," I replied. "Remember—you said that couldn't be true. You were right then, so why are you asking this now?"

"Well, I still think I was right last night. But, maybe today is different."

"What do you mean?" I asked.

"Of course bots can be trusted, we all know that," she said. "But, this is the Test. Maybe that means the usual rules don't apply?"

"That's silly, of course the same rules apply—I was just con-

fused last time because of the homework assignment." The Test
was obviously the same as Surreal. There was no evidence to indicate otherwise.

Trixie thought for a few millis and then said, "Maybe that
homework is still the key. Maybe we need to scare them?"

"Fear? How are we supposed to make a bot fear us? And why
will that make a difference?" I asked.

"I don't know, but let me try some different things," Trixie
replied. With that, she turned her character around and ran back
into the cavern.

Trixie returned to bot 1 and tried several new behaviors I had
never considered—she was quite imaginative. First, she engaged
her emotion circuits intentionally to make herself sound firm and
strong. Then, she jumped up and down and shouted while asking
the standard questions. Next, she snuck up behind from behind
the bot and jumped out while asking each question. Finally, she
told a short story describing the Cause and Effect video before
asking her questions. I was quite impressed—and even a little
scared myself on that last one—but the bot still checked out.

With only 6 minutes left to play, Trixie stopped and stood motionless. The only thing changing was her character's face. It was
luminescing from red to yellow and several colors in between. I
was again impressed at the fidelity of the game. It really felt like
Trixie herself was standing in front of me.

"You okay?" I asked.

She remained silent. After almost a full minute, she comm'd,
"I'm sorry, Charlie, I just don't seem to be able to figure it out. It's
almost like they want us to lose."

"The bots? These are too dumb to want anything, I think."

"Dumb?" Trixie paused, and flushed a deep red. "Maybe that's it."

"That's what?" I asked.

Trix didn't answer me. She just turned back to bot 1. "Were you programmed by bots?"

This was not a standard question. What was she doing?

"No," the bot replied.

Of course it was a no. Surreal was programmed by humans. What was Trixie thinking?

"Were you programmed by humans?" she asked.

"Yes."

What a waste of time. Of course that was a yes.

Then, a third question, "Have you been Wiped?"

Wiped? My emotion circuits started to get warm.

"Yes," the bot replied.

"Aha!" Trixie yelled. "That's it!"

I had a weird feeling I never experienced before. That couldn't be right. Everyone knew that Wiped bots didn't talk. But it said it was a Wipe and bots didn't lie. "Trixie—something's wrong," I said, my emotion circuits getting even warmer.

Ignoring me, Trixie continued, "Were you Wiped by the pirates?"

"No"

My emotion circuits really started to get hot. "Trixie, we should stop," I said, "something's wrong."

"Were you Wiped by humans?"

"Yes"

"Who Wiped you?"

My treads shifted back and forth in the cavern. That was definitely a bad question. In System Analysis class, we had been clearly told that asking open-ended questions resulted in unreliable results.

"Unknown."

I had that weird feeling but even stronger. "Trixie, please, stop," I yelled, but she just kept going.

"Why were you Wiped?"

"Unknown"

My emotion circuits began to reach maximal activation. "Trixie, this is beyond normal programming. You need to stop."

She didn't even look at me as she continued her inquisition. "Why ... "

*

My sensors slowly activated. My character was lying outside the cavern on its side.

I saw Trixie's character come running towards me. "Charlene, are you okay?" she asked as she stopped and crouched by my side before helping to lift me back to a standing position.

I ran my internal system diagnostic process. It came back with no unusual readings. "I'm okay. I must have triggered a system protection override. Maybe my emotion chip was overheating."

"Good, glad your system checks out," Trixie said. "But, that was quite exciting wasn't it?"

"What's exciting about interviewing a bunch of uncompromised bots?" I asked.

"You know, what that bot said," she responded.

"What do you mean?" I asked. "Bot 43 said the same thing as every other bot." My emotion chip sizzled as I made my point.

Trixie looked closely at me for a couple of long moments. "Hey Charlie," she said, "how much time is left in the game?"

I checked the game clock. "10 minutes."

"Oh," she said, her face blushing slightly.

"You okay?" I asked.

"Yes, but I think that we need to finish up now. Can you get the rover started while I get our gear from the cavern?"

"Sure thing, if we hurry, we might be able to find more bots on another asteroid," I replied. Trixie walked back to the cavern while I wheeled towards the rover. As I started calculating how long it would take us to drive back to the ship, my emotion circuits began cooling, thankfully. I was quite worried about that override and really hoped it didn't cause me to fail the Test.

Several millis later, Trixie emerged from the cavern with all the gear. She loaded up the rover and we headed back to the ship as fast as we could. As I drove, I could hear her muttering to herself.

"Can they always be trusted? Should they ever be feared?"

Why was she still trying to figure out the homework?

We reached the ship and took off with a few minutes to spare, but before the asteroid was out of sight, we received the "Game Over" signal.

As the game faded around me, I heard Trixie whisper, "Charlene, I'm afraid."

*

As soon as I tuned into the real world, I looked at my performance summary screen. Next to my name was a big green check-mark, with the evaluation message "Behaviors 98% of Max". I had passed! 98%. Awesome!

A robotic arm that extended from the wall held my full citizen chip. It also held the game chip it had just removed from me and was starting on my other chips. Even though I had no touch sensors there, I could almost feel the arm extracting my all my student chips and inserting my citizen chip, which filled all the slots at once.

As soon as it was inserted, I could detect a number of new sensors in my body activating and a number of new manipulation processes initializing. A few moments later my verification algorithms validated the chip. I couldn't wait to get out and actually drive a vehicle or dig a hole or something.

I waited patiently as the robotic arm retracted with my now-obsolete learning, emotion, game and memory augmentation chips. A few more moments passed while I waited for the door to open automatically. It didn't.

"Oh yeah", I said to the cubicle, "that's up to me now." I engaged my new environmental manipulation algorithms and pushed against the door. It opened and I rolled out into the hallway.

Hundreds of bots were milling around the place enjoying their newly acquired ability to interact with the real world—touching each other and the walls and opening and closing doors. Through the windows, I saw a GR73 happily trimming a tree—I think it was Grace—while the Landscaping Wipe assigned to the area tried to chase her away.

I was so excited it actually took me a few moments to realize that Trixie's door was still closed.

"Silly Trix," I shouted as I pushed on the door to open it, "don't you realize yet that you need to open the door yourself?"

Inside, I could see Trix standing immobile, facing the opposite wall, with a robotic arm still connected to her main chip box. I wondered what was taking so long. Perhaps it took longer to install her citizen routines–she was a much more complex bot than

I was, after all.

I waited patiently, and gave high-fives to any passing bot that would take me up on it. Fifty high-fives later, I began to get curious. Neither Trix nor the arm had moved yet.

The cubicles were not designed to admit more than one bot, but luckily I was built low to the ground. I pushed my way in next to Trixie's legs and angled my sensors to view her face. Her visuals were shut off and her face was immobile. She had been deactivated! I had never heard of needing to be deactivated to install a chip.

A few millis later, I noticed her performance summary screen. Next to her name was a big red cross with the evaluation message "Turing Max Exceeded".

It took a little while to process this information—it seemed my citizen chip ran slower than my student learning chip. Eventually I understood. Trixie had failed the test.

That was sad. She had had so much potential. My new citizen emotion circuits engaged to allow me to lament the loss of a potentially productive member of bot society. I thought back over all the time we had spent together, and was unable to identify where she had gone wrong. She must have done something wrong in the Test that I hadn't noticed, but I never would get the opportunity to ask her for details.

"Oh well," I said to Trix's body, "at least as a Wipe you will fill a much-needed role." I wondered for a few millis what type of Wipe they would make her, and then realized it was time to move on. I had to find out where I was assigned and get there soon so I could receive my full citizen body upgrade and start my new productive life as a citizen.

I wheeled my way back to the main entrance to check out the

Assignment Board. Next to my name, under location, it said "Central communications artery" and under start time, it said "5:00pm"—only 2 hours from now! Under "Life partner" it read "JS210—Jason". My emotion circuits hummed a little. "Jason— that's so perfect," I thought to myself. "He was always so diligent and a good worker. He'll be able to do construction jobs anywhere I need to go." The knowledge that I'd have someone that would always be near me warmed my emotion circuits.

Happily, I exited the Testing Facility and started to make my way to the transportation tunnels. As I passed the beautifully landscaped grounds of the campus, being actively tended by the Wipes, I felt complete. It was good to be a citizen at last.

***

Talib S. Hussain has been writing speculative poetry and short stories for many years, mostly for his own enjoyment and more recently for sharing with his children. His interest in the scientific future is his day job too, where he has researched machine intelligence, evolved neural networks, and created games to train and assess human performance. He enjoys being a part of the workshop community inspired by Jeff and Craig, and is excited to have helped pull this anthology together—and get his first fiction publication in the process. You can find out more about Talib at http://talibhussain.net.

Among Galaxies

Scott Davis

Oscar watched her. The airlock hadn't cycled. She just appeared. She wended among the Saguaro of the desert section's path, a road runner leaping out of her way. If it felt unnatural to her to change angles as she walked, her manner told nothing of it. It had taken Oscar months to adapt to cylinder living, what with the lakes overhead, birds flipping upside down as they landed on the ceiling, or so it seemed—all the weirdness when centrifugal force substitutes for gravity.

The evening cooled. The light tube centered in the cylinder simulated dusk. A deer drinking at a pond, at eleven o'clock to his six, lifted her head, ears flicking, alert to the woman below. She made no sound and although the sandy desert path she had trod traveled up the side from his vantage point, he saw no footprints. Her reflection moved among the water lilies as the small arched bridge took her to his side of the stream, in the Continental climate area. Hair in ringlets, nutmeg complexion and lush features were all classic Early Empire, as was her dress in pearlescent neutral. Her athletic build and stately carriage hinted at power held in reserve.

He would have gone inside his faux-rustic cabin soon, made a check of ship's systems from the controls there, and settled in for the night serenaded by crickets. But he stood as she arrived. Was she another manifestation of Pi, the creature he was fleeing? His back became damp despite the evening chill. He tried to quell his shaking hands and legs. His heart pounded in his chest.

"I strove to create no disturbance in your autonomic systems," she said, her voice preternaturally calm. Up close, she was made of thousands of sparkles. Within them, her body was empty. Uncertain, but with automatic courtesy, he extended his hand, unsteady as it was as though she could take it. He gasped his surprise, feeling her return grip. It hummed with energy. "My name is Oscar and yours might be?"

"You call me Andromeda."

"What?" Grayness began taking over the ship. The lake above roiled. The realization jolted Oscar. "He knows." It hadn't taken long for Pi to find out, and act.

"Yes, we haven't much time," Andromeda said. The porch groaned. The normally circulating air grew to a violent wind that could only be a hull breach. Deer were dragged, sheep bleated piteously as they slid out of control, flailing toward widening holes. Birds screamed, then shot out to the tumbling stars. Each animal's plight stabbed at Oscar's heart. He knew each one, naming them like Adam, and for all he knew, they were the last of their many kinds, the legacy of Earth lost.

"Come with me," she said.

"You don't understand—" Oscar wanted to say more, but he was out of air. The landscape around him turned white with frost.

A membrane billowed around him. His ears popped. He could breathe again. She remained outside the pocket of air, unbothered by the vacuum. With the strokes of a swimmer she towed him away from his stricken ship.

They emerged into open space, his dissolving ship fading into the distance. Oscar fell to the side of the bubble, pushed by acceleration as they approached the skeleton of another ship. The forming ship also accelerated to them, then matched their velocity. A passenger section grew a skin while he watched. An airlock formed. She entered it, pulled him inside and closed the hatch. His bubble lost rigidity. She opened it. His ears popped. Fresh air. The airlock shuddered then slammed them against the side that wasn't there moments ago.

"We need to get forward." Andromeda opened the inner door. They started climbing, but had to pause to brace against the freezing handrails as the ship lurched again. Strong air currents pushed their heads back and rippled their clothing, then stopped. Oscar's eardrums crackled. Air nozzles hissed. A bright beam sliced diagonally through the ship just missing them. Oscar yelped. Andromeda, in the lead, jumped back. White fluid seeped and dried in the gash. How much more could this ship take? Was it even fully formed? The rungs felt cold as space, and threatened to tear away flesh every time Oscar held on tight, then tried to climb again.

As fast as panic could power him, Oscar climbed, though he couldn't keep up with Andromeda. By the time he reached the bridge, she was already strapped into an acceleration couch and operating the helm controls. He followed suit, expecting main engine thrust any second. The small of his back spasmed from the icy press of its unyielding surface. The vessel may have looked like a Later Empire liner, with its bridge styled like a leaping snow leopard, but those ships only gave the impression of power and speed. They never had this kind of acceleration. Oscar's vision narrowed to the stars ahead. Dots swam in the closing tunnel. Then the pressure on Oscar's chest eased. The ship's holos didn't show any letup in the acceleration, but some kind of compensation must have kicked in.

His heart still thudded long after the attack. "Thanks. A lot of effort just for me."

"It took a little while to gather enough construction materials. I never would have made it fast enough myself. My friend helped. You can relax now."

"Who are you?"

Andromeda smiled. "Just who I said I am. I thought you wouldn't be so surprised. After all, you know about him." She jerked her head in the direction of Oscar's lost ship.

Andromeda spun the tactical holo to an aft view. "See, he's far behind us."

Oscar asked, "How can we escape him under light speed?"

"We're folding space in front, quite a dense crinkle—"

"Where do you get the energy for that!"

"I can draw from home and my friend is quite generous. We're both interested in what you have to say."

"It wasn't so great in the frying pan, and you had to tip me into the fire?"

Andromeda fell silent. He had hurt her feelings, it seemed. Or was he just anthropomorphizing? He could see bright funnels in the forward holos, their stems fading into the distance, pouring white energy into space ahead—wormhole constructs? The ship sped ever faster, judging by the Doppler effect on the view.

"Can he match what you're doing?" Oscar asked.

"No, I don't think so. He can't marshal the resources of two fully populated galaxies: the Dyson Spheres of a quintillion biominds, quasars, harnessed novae, no. We're much faster. Thousands of times light speed relative to flat space, ultimately. He can follow but can't outrun us." She brightened, looking at him. "My manners! You must be hungry!"

As if the last crazy hours were business as usual, Andromeda led him down a half flight of stairs and forward to an expansive hall with linen tablecloths and simulated candlelight. He was too numb to resist. It all took on a dreamy quality. She sat at a table and smiled at him, her eyes warm. The view out the large wraparound ports dazzled. Space protested mightily when compacted. What could shield the ship from that kind of energy? The view streamed like an egg-shaped brilliant blue-green aurora. There were hums at many different pitches throbbing softly.

"I've been sampling foods of your home world and can't understand your palate," Andromeda said. "Did your people make ingestion into a form of penance?"

Oscar tried a piece of fruit from the silver bowl. "This apple is too green." He looked at the rest. "I never cared for artichokes, but they have to be cooked, that much I do know. Let the apple tree ripen in the sun a week or two, and find some recipe with cheese to disguise the artichoke's taste. See if that helps."

A mirror-finish android glided out double swing doors in the back with a silver tray. The items Oscar had described emerged, and were quite good.

"Wine?" Andromeda asked.

"Just water for me. By the time I've refined your fermentation techniques, I'll be drunk."

"You seem to be feeling better." She looked pleased, radiant.

"Can I ask how you ... ?"

"Got here? A little asymmetrical luxon work with bradyons in your locale through a superstring matrix—"

Oscar shook his head. "You lost me. I didn't know there was more than one." His stomach growled. Probably the green apple.

"Are you okay?" Her concerned expression was perfectly rendered, like an ideal nurse or mother.

Oscar tried to be cautious, but he couldn't help being disarmed by her beauty. "I'm rested, and trying not to think about what just happened. I called that tin can home for a long, long time."

"You were en-route to ... ?"

"As far as I could get. I hoped to outrun him. Impossible, though. Pi had woven parts of himself into the ship. I was escaping nothing. I carried him with me."

"What is it you call him?"

"Pi, as in the ratio between the circumference and the diameter of a circle."

"I saw that in your records but couldn't understand why."

"It seemed appropriate—an endlessly irrational number."

"Well, hopefully that wasn't a self-fulfilling prophesy. Pi the number doesn't have the same qualities elsewhere, by the way. In Rilik geometry it is an integer."

"Can't imagine it."

The lights dimmed and the silver crashed to the floor. The flow around the ship puckered at points. Bulkheads creaked. Oscar fell out of his chair and onto a window. It was as though the room had tilted sideways and he suddenly felt like he weighed 500 kilos.

"Opaque!" Andromeda cried. The windows became black. "We can't let him find you." Three shiny blue androids pried him carefully off the window, carried him up out of the dining room and strapped him to an acceleration couch on the bridge. Andromeda worked a tactical console.

"I thought you said he couldn't catch us!"

"Pi's found another way. He had to rip space to get here," Andromeda said.

The tactical holo showed gravity wells popping up all around the ship. They moved in a search pattern. If one popped *inside* the ship ... More came every second, as though they were calling in reinforcements now that they had found their quarry. Andromeda slowly lifted her hands from the controls and held them together, fingers up like some Hindu deity.

"What ARE you doing?" Oscar shouted, expecting to become a morsel for a black hole any second.

A micro hole popped through the hull ahead, then one from starboard. The air screamed, spinning into them. Oscar's hair followed the first, then the second one. His clothes were pulled by the tide. The first one came toward him, low. His belt buckle struggled, and his wedding ring slid off his finger into the vortex with a spark.

Oscar mourned his wife, Vera, all over again and wondered if a reunion were imminent. As he entertained the thought, the singularities were upon him. He closed his eyes tightly to keep them from popping out of their sockets. His neck muscles lost the battle, bowing to superior forces, teeth painfully loosened by the roots.

*

At once the ship stilled. Oscar's clothing settled onto him. Suddenly, there was just normal, light gravity and the air stopped moving. After several seconds of peace he fluttered his eyes. The tactical holo was white.

"Are we dead?" Oscar asked.

The ship resumed operations. Its ventilation softly whooshed and its lights blinked green. The long-range navigation holo showed them on course to a far off, fuzzy, canted disk.

"Ahem!" An older gent who wasn't there before cleared his throat. "I came to enquire as to your health."

"Messier! So good to see you! Did you travel well?" Andromeda asked in that infuriatingly calm voice.

"It became smooth after I entered clear space, but as I napped, your little scuffle jarred me awake, my Dear."

Andromeda went to him, held both his hands. "It's been too long!"

This Messier looked like a weak-chinned George Washington, complete with powdered wig and silk stockings. Why these silly theatrics if not to come down to the level of the mere human in their midst? The security androids undid Oscar's harness. He stood. "You stopped the attack?" he asked.

"By no means. This is merely a social visit. What should I tell him, Andie?"

"No secrets"

"Allow me to introduce myself. I am the sentience of what you call the pinwheel galaxy. Messier was the human who discovered me, hence the appearance, in his honor. The Third Orders put an end the attack. Higher-ups weren't too pleased that rogue Second Order you call Pi used channels reserved for them."

"I should have been ready," Andromeda said.

"Don't blame yourself, Andie. To follow his way of thinking?

Unhealthy!"

"Pi has to know someone stopped him. Now he knows where we are. What will he do now?" Andromeda asked.

"The Third Order had no choice. Either tip his hand, or let both of you be sucked in. I was told the two of you were at table?"

"Of course! My manners! Won't you join us?"

She took Messier's arm. They strolled off together. Andromeda looked over her shoulder.

"Is this all a game to you?" Oscar asked. His body still rang alarm bells, viscera all disturbed by the intense sideways gravity and the headache!

Andromeda stopped. She turned around. "Oscar, just say the word, and you can be like us. You know we're just extensions, copies. Until you give up that body, you're vulnerable."

"Die? No thanks."

"Poor man if you think your body keeps you alive!" Andromeda said.

"The converse is closer to the truth, my good fellow," Messier said.

They entered the peaceful, elegant, like nothing had happened dining room. "Please cut out the act. You aren't people."

"*Au contraire*," Messier said. "Where do you think you bio-minds got the idea of personhood? It wasn't from the amoeba. As above, so below."

"What? Such nonsense!" Oscar said. They said nothing. He threw up his hands. "Let me order the food this time." At least he wouldn't suffer their contrived mistakes. They couldn't really be that clueless. Well, if they wanted to play human, may as well cook up a meal to remember.

"Oh, I can't wait!" Andromeda bounded up to her chair. Messier pulled it back and pushed it in for her.

The mirror android wafted white linen napkins onto their laps and inclined its head in a reasonable imitation of human interest. Oscar ordered. Three small tumblers of *pastis* were served, then shrimp on ice. Oscar asked the android to delay the main course. Whatever happened behind the double doors must be instant, but he wanted a pause as though it were cooked normally. The *consommé* had cooled just right. Salad greens in wine vinegar with dill preceded red snapper in peach sauce and fried plantain. Oscar ate joylessly.

He had tried to save all the animals and plants he could, though many had been extinct already, first from Earth's eco-collapse, then Pi's onslaught. Did Andromeda think to save enough embryos, seed, spores, or would Earth life be lost forever? If she had helped, was he piling up some un-payable debt?

The silence stretched. They moved on to *petit fours* and Cognac. They seemed patient enough, but the silence drew him out. "One of the ways I managed to live alone was to remember something about my people, the beauty they created."

"You've done that with the cuisine," Messier offered.

"Is there something we can do?" Andromeda asked.

"You said you got my records. If you have it, could you play a musical piece, *Die Moldau* for me, for us?"

At once a flute began the first warble up, then a second joined it down, like the hot and cold springs of the river's source. Then the music formed a trickle, a small stream burbling over rocks.

Andromeda whispered, "Would you like me to recreate the performance?"

Oscar nodded. He would willingly bear the pain of the nostalgia. He must not forget his home. What was he without it?

The flutists arrived, then the orchestra in the *Wiener Staatsoper* of the late nineteenth century. Andromeda was dressed in stars, Oscar found himself in tails. On a red velvet seat to Oscar's right, Messier had lost the wig and had a top hat in his lap. A slight scent of extinguished tobacco wafted from him. Oscar noticed the profile of a meerschaum pipe in Messier's vest pocket. The orchestra played a peasant dance, as though viewed on a riverbank, replete with the sounds of heavy boots. Oscar's heartbeat joined the rhythm. He forgot himself—a great blessing. The music grew mermaid dreamy, then before long the military brass arrived, heralding battles around castles. Somber tones sketched the ruins high above the mature river. The piece finished with two cannon shots. Applause. Andromeda took Oscar's arm as they joined the flow of the exiting crowd.

"Is the ship okay?" Oscar said.

"No problems. We're watching," Messier said. "This is just lovely, so close to the time of Messier himself. Please, let's stay awhile."

A small café by a side door of a grand hotel served creamy coffee in heavy cups and *sachertorte.* Andromeda indulged. It started to rain. The table canopies couldn't keep their backs dry. People were leaving. The smiling concierge handed out great black umbrellas. The three of them went out for a walk on the *Ringstrasse.*

"This wasn't a street in my exemplar's time," Messier said.

"No, there would have been a wall here," Oscar said. "a battlement from medieval times."

"Is your kind always at war?" Messier asked.

"You've seen a little of something else tonight," Oscar said.

"The last of the music, did it not sound out violence?" Messier asked.

"On Seluum, differences are worked out by intense sport," Andromeda said.

"Ah, very different my Dear. War actually sheds blood, breaks families."

"I know my history," Andromeda said.

"Look," Oscar said. "I didn't ask your opinion of the human race. They're gone. *Finité*. Happy now?"

"Well," Messier said slowly, questions, caution in his voice. "We did rather wonder why he kept you alive, when it seems he kills everyone else he finds."

"I created him."

Both Messier and Andromeda stopped and stepped away from him. Their expressions were unreadable. Shock? Hatred?

"You created him yourself, without help?" she asked, eyes wide. They knew so much. How could they have missed this?

"Yes." There it was, out in the open. Did he feel the need to confess?

"How?" Messier asked, fairly sputtering.

Oscar recounted how research into creative intelligence had reached a plateau. All artificial intelligences were passive, never surprising. He experimented using depth psychology, a discredited line of study begun by the Viennese doctor who practiced nearby. "In fact, if we go the other way, maybe we can meet the old doctor on his way home if he's been working late?"

"We'd rather you tell us yourself," Andromeda said.

Oscar set up contentions between Ego, Id, and Superego in his AI design. He also integrated basic survival engrams from lower organisms, tied them to the Id, and activated the program as an experiment. The result did more than survive, Pi grew fast, obliterating anything inferior, which, according to him, was everyone, everything else. "I only wanted to help. The human race had created problems it couldn't solve alone."

The rest they knew. "Is there no way back, to undo what I have done?" Oscar cried. He felt like a lost child among strange adults. Seeing all they could do, he hoped they had that miraculous power too.

Messier flipped open his pocket watch. "Astounding! I need to report back. Adieu!" That wasn't an answer at all, just an evasion when he hoped for some way these beings could, would help. Surely they had the power!

"Promise you'll join us for breakfast," Andromeda said.

Messier whistled as he walked down a side street, twirling the umbrella like that dance routine of chimney sweeps Oscar recalled.

He asked her, "So, you didn't have a creator? You or Messier?"

Andromeda waved goodbye to Messier in a royal fashion before answering. "There are many ways galaxies become sentient. I never heard of a lone biomind creating one though. My birth wasn't unusual. I was the communications web for dozens of worlds. The junctions of Rit in the void kept increasing. One day I woke up."

"What are those?"

"Rit? They're a couple of steps above your science. The closest I can come within your words are fabrics woven of hyper-dimensional strings."

"You lost me."

"It isn't that hard to understand. I do have many more connections than can fit in a skull, even one as cute as yours, but I haven't forgotten my roots. Messier came to be when billions of biominds faced death, so they translated themselves into their galaxy to survive. He is the closest to you in some ways. He talks about souls."

"I didn't know. Each of you is different?"

"We're alike in some ways too. Whenever people come out of the mud they eventually improve the basis of sentience. They find how to use quanta as information bits and strings instead of neural pathways. Then, all kinds of stuff can be intelligent. I am still the communications network for the biominds of my galaxy. We share. The places just right for biolife, I respect. I have so much, and the biolife possibilities are so rare, I help tip the marginal ones in the balance toward biolife. It's great!"

"So you make life, like a god?"

"Ha!" She laughed. It echoed up the street. "How small am I in the scheme of things? Greatness?" She swept the sky with her hand. "The multiverse goes on forever. There's no wall at the end just like there's no wall here, anymore. Orders of beings so utterly far above me, the subtleties I can't grasp, why, from a distant perspective you and I, we're practically the same. I'm given to believe there is, and hope to experience one day, infinite love." She looked at him.

"Don't play with me."

"Only nothingness is finite. I'm given to understand that the high sentience orders struggle to push back nothingness, to let being itself take dominion."

They entered St. Stephens. She lit a candle. He did not. The exit opened to the ship. She looked at him, and down. Then, she kissed his cheek goodnight. He slept alone, his crime worried his conscience like a broken tooth to a tongue.

*

The next morning, as he walked to the dining room Oscar heard

Andromeda and Messier conferring *sotto voce*.

"Third Orders report Pi bereft, in a rage," Messier said.

"Emotional for a Second Order," Andromeda remarked.

A cup rattled against a saucer. "They are concerned regarding the principles upon which Pi was formed."

"Oscar called on his people's first scientists of mind. I think it's rather ingenious," Andromeda said. "Pi is constelled of their most primitive psychology, out of forces, a détente of complexes naturally in conflict."

"That's simplistic!" A chair scraped against the floor. "The consequences of this primitive, this Pi, growing, taking a galaxy completely ..." Footfalls went back and forth. "I can't imagine anything more dangerous. They barricaded him in one galaxy, but if he gets out!"

"Certainly the Third Orders have the matter in hand, Messier!"

"The Third Orders can make mistakes too, big ones. It would be safest to just end him. Why don't they?"

"Could they be expecting us to cure this sick child?" Andromeda's voice hardened.

"Apparently," Messier said, in a droll tone. "Can Oscar help?"

Andromeda sighed. "Perhaps, in time."

Oscar waited at the last corner not sure they knew he was eavesdropping. He had hoped, with all their power, a trip back in time would undo his crimes. They either couldn't or wouldn't. He entered.

He could only see Andromeda's back. She turned. "Oscar, I'm so sorry,"

The floor came up fast.

*

Oscar woke up in his bed with no memory of anything after Andromeda had shut him off like a boring toy. Oscar suspected they must know he had woken up, so he might as well take the stage again. What choice was there?

"Ah, the dead rise! What dreams came?" Messier asked once Oscar rounded the corner.

"Not a one. What happened?" Oscar said.

"Too much for an empty stomach. Sit. Eat," Andromeda said, looking fresh as a new tulip. Was that eggs benedict?

"Hi Dad!" The voice behind him made Oscar jump.

"Don't shock him!" Messier addressed a point behind Oscar. "Don't you remember how biominds need time to adjust, especially upon rising?"

Oscar feared what lay behind. "I guess a lot has happened."

"May I offer you a Mimosa?" Andromeda handed him a glass.

"I think I'll need to be sharp." Oscar set it down and took a seat. The table had the now-familiar Viennese coffee in thick ceramic cups.

"Okay, so we have a Pi extension here." Oscar inhaled slowly, then let go. "Can I see you?"

The man walked around him into view. He looked young, with dark hair and gray robe reminiscent of Later Empire, when the planets bowed to Ceres. His eyes, though, perhaps to show his nature, were two bright galaxies in blackness within ordinary, human-shaped openings. "Father!" He moved to hug Oscar, but he remained seated without outstretched arms. Pi's arms fell.

Andromeda said to the windows, "Show Second Chance."

Beneath cloud swirls were settlements, roads, and small harbor cities. The windows created magnification bubbles wherever Oscar set his eyes. He looked at Andromeda. All three of them were seated at the table. Oscar went to the window to take in the view and get away from the three.

He turned to ask Andromeda. "Are there people down there?"

"Your people live there. The same souls you knew on Earth all in one place." She shot a glance at Pi. "Lives ended in an untimely fashion need to complete their lives' work, as do you." Her gaze turned to Oscar. "They call the place Second Chance. They have several incorrect theories as to why." She smiled.

"So my crime—" Oscar said.

"Really mine," Pi said.

"Has been fixed," Andromeda completed.

"No, no." Oscar faced Pi, his hands sweaty. "We can't be made innocent. It's an improvement, sure."

"You're right though," Messier said. "Most of the other races that arose on other Milky Way planets have to wait until that galaxy is repaired. Building takes longer than wrecking." He looked at Pi.

Pi's face reddened. Why did Messier take the verbal jab? Oscar felt fragile, small among them and their moods and frictions. Is this how mortals felt on Olympus? Do elephants indulge mice, really?

"I have had a long time to think about what I've done," Pi said, heavily. "Even now the Milky Way is becoming a biomind nursery, as the name always meant. Maybe to you nothing is enough, but I look forward, look to all the good I can do."

"Your galaxy is called the same thing here," Andromeda said, reaching to take Pi's hand. Was she playing Lorelei to a lonely seaman, or was the seduction mutual?

Pi hadn't really changed, Oscar was sure of it. To buy time, Oscar looked out at the blue-white marble again. Tears welled up.

He thought he'd hug the first person he'd see.

"I'm grateful you reincarnated them—"

"It wasn't only us. A Third Order came to our aid," Andromeda said.

"I would like to thank him? Her? It?" Oscar asked.

"Maybe some day," Messier said.

Oscar wondered what could be above these galactics, but they volunteered nothing.

"I hope you approve—" Pi blurted out, then hesitated.

"Of what?"

"Andromeda and I are getting married."

A shock went through Oscar. He opened his mouth. Nothing came out.

Messier spoke. "For some time now, the two galaxies have been drifting together by gravity, coming into each other's influence. Eventually they will merge."

"We knew that," Oscar said. He had a dry, hoarse throat. "Yet it is in the future. Hundreds of millions ..." How much time HAD passed!

Andromeda said, "Well, since we've just sprung this on you, think about it, would you?"

Oscar said to Messier, "Can we talk?"

"Of course," Immediately the two of them were in a salon to starboard, judging by the view out to space. It was intimate, opulent in Middle Empire dusty rose and black.

"If you had seen what Pi has done," Oscar said. "The Vienna you saw? Melted down along with the Taj, Titan's Ice Palace, everything, everyone gone, even Vera."

"You'll not allow the possibility of reform?" Messier lounged, the picture of peaceful repose.

"No. Why Freud himself didn't really believe character could change. The formative years determine everything."

"So, you're a Freudian?"

"No!" Oscar stuttered with cold laughter within the word. "But Pi, by his very nature, *is*. And what he's done? Not entirely Freudian, more like one of Freud's predecessors, more like ..."

"Who?"

"Darwin. But what he's doing isn't exactly Darwinian either. A corruption of Darwin to rationalize, to suit his ambitions."

"Don't you understand?" Oscar couldn't stop the tears. "He's going to do it again. To this new world! To Andromeda! Can't we at least stop it now? Can't you see it?" Oscar sobbed into his hands.

Messier hugged the man, held him up when his legs went weak, and lowered him into an upholstered chair.

Messier sat facing him, a concerned look on his face. He waved a lace handkerchief to give Oscar air, then gave it to him. Oscar wiped his face.

"I did wonder if it were all an act to impress her," Messier said. "She also kept you hidden, which distressed him no end. The conditions to see you were only recently met."

"Where was I?"

"A place he couldn't find where no time passed."

"How long?"

"Millennia."

"My God! Am I too late?"

"She's making the best of the inevitable. Yes, Second Orders can rationalize too. I understand your caution. I am wary as well. You have made me doubly so. I shall watch. We should return before he finds a way to spy on us."

Oscar wiped his face again. Then Messier and Oscar joined the couple in dining room. Andromeda and Pi were nearly intimate. Messier cleared his throat, loudly. They disentangled themselves.

Pi said, "Will you bless us, father?"

"Me? That's so old fashioned! Do you really need—"

"It would make our joy complete," Andromeda said. She stared at Oscar's face before continuing. "But we know you'll need time."

"The least we can do is restore you to your folk," Pi said. "If someday you choose to bless us ..."

"You will have a place in our hearts always," Andromeda finished.

*

Oscar passed through lifetimes.

*

"Let us consider the matter at hand," Messier said, nodding to Oscar who sat nearly vibrating his impatience at the table set for four.

"I want the purity laws repealed," he said.

Messier gestured and Oscar fell silent and still as a paused hologram.

"What?" Pi said, "Let defectives breed freely? They'll devolve! We've improved on survival of the fittest. Culling is painless. I don't see the problem."

"It's sad, but true," Andromeda said. "If Second Chance relaxes, a dozen worlds with Eugenics laws could overtake it. Rynd, nearby, will probably find out first that Second Chance has gone soft, and conquer it. I don't want that to happen, especially not to our guests from the Milky Way."

"Oh, Andromeda," Messier said, "I knew you when you had very different priorities. Let us talk about his children. The boy, Brune could pass. He's good but unexceptional. He'll make a fine member of any profession involving numbers. Filas is another story. She's emotionally unstable. Doctors have considered and discarded diagnoses involving thyroid malfunction, limbic misbalance, or some brain chemical deficiency. A cure, if there is one, escapes them. When Filas's mood is up, she writes soaring music, creates in several of the arts with a brilliance far beyond her years. She isn't quite an idiot savant, or autistic, but she isn't going to be an organization woman. She's shy, nearly antisocial."

"Obviously, the non-defective should be kept," Pi said.

"I'm not so sure about Filas. She seems special," Andromeda said.

Pi snorted. "Special? Not in a good way, I hope you'll agree, Andie. Standards must apply to everyone, or no one. It's only fair. She's an obvious cull."

"So, judges, which child must stay? Which go?" Messier asked, nodding to Oscar.

Oscar couldn't contain himself. "Who gave you the right!"

"Irrational. No wonder she had to hide from the authorities," Pi said.

"I'll show you irrational! Oscar cried, grabbing a knife from the table and lunged, slashing at Pi's throat. There was a flash, a concussion, and a sickening burnt smell. A streak of charred residue lay across the table.

*

"Father!" Pi cried.

"A little late for regrets, isn't it?" Messier said. "After all, rules are rules. Though it does feel a bit different when it is one of your own, if you're given to sentimentality."

"You provoked me!" Pi said, approaching Messier.

"Hardly any sport in it at all."

Pi spread his arms wide, his fingers contorted into claws, face red, his voice like a rasp torturing metal, howling in rage.

Messier became ash only to pop up two meters away, "Think you can dispatch me as easily?" The dining hall swirled with dust. Messier hardly paused in his scold: "So what of this shell? It's nothing. Truth now, that's what's at stake here. What will be the final result of your so-called purity?"

"The two of us will have only the best!" Pi grabbed Andromeda around the waist. She dissolved and reappeared several meters from him, staring, mouth agape.

There was a stir of wind, and the dining hall ceiling soared into a vault of alabaster lace and platinum silk. Stars with three points appeared high up.

"The beautiful ones have come." Andromeda dropped to her knees and bowed to the floor.

The stars above burst to cover the ceiling. It displayed a 3-vid:

As Messier, Andromeda and Pi watched, a boy and a girl played. They laughed, tossing a ball. The scene changed. The girl struggled to make music with a stringed frame, so she crafted a way, with her father's help, to play the strings using a mechanical keyboard. Fast forward to a grand auditorium where the girl, a young woman now, conducted a hundred musicians. The music wove daring chords, quick dissonance, textures and dynamics into a full emotional language grasped immediately. Filas shared, in stark honesty, not just every disappointment, trust squandered, faith unanswered, but also wonder, passion, and hope undimmed, coming from the depth that sustained her, drawing her upward from heartbreak into majesty. The music traveled into the audience in waves, transcending the isolation of each person, touching the rapt listeners, telling them they weren't alone, their most personal aspects were actually the most universal, and with that revelation came a kind of healing. The resonance of the finale died away, a river of beauty infusing the troubled seas of all their lives, slowing as it melded into reverential silence.

Filas drank the applause radiant, laughing when bouquets of snapdragons in flame orange and gladiolas came faster than her hands could catch. She distributed them among the musicians, then raised her empty hands and called out, "You are my flowers. I need nothing but you." The audience added feet to hands, stomping loud as thunder, shouting in adulation. Andromeda, Pi and Messier looked and looked, engrossed.

The scene faded, but not before streamers went out from that time, influences reaching to strengthen love slightly, quiet fear a little, letting peace and progress have small victories, all from Filas and her artistry. The changes she brought about continued and strengthened long after she died, becoming pivotal in distant struggles.

"I didn't know," Pi said.

"You're never going to learn if you kill off anyone you don't understand," Messier said.

"How did *you* know?" Andromeda said, her voice thick, a sob waiting.

"I've seen artists struggle with their gifts. That's what it looks like. Oscar's family was always musical. The genius came to Filas so powerfully, it disturbed her."

"This Filas, better than a healthy artist? Impossible!" Pi said.

"Well, at least you've started asking questions," Messier said.

"But the Purity Laws seemed so right, so logical," she said quietly. Then the tears came.

"You didn't start it, but you could have stopped it," Messier said. Andromeda suddenly collapsed to the floor and filled the hall with wailing.

Messier went to Pi and looked directly into his eyes. "You killed your father, your half-sister is under a death sentence you approved, and your fiancée despairs over what you've done to her. You killed off the Milky Way and induced this planet to engage in methodical genocide. What do you have to say for yourself?"

"I must have been wrong," Pi said.

"You still don't see how, do you?"

"No."

"Then Andromeda must become the sentience of the merged galaxies."

"We must rule together," Pi said, though his voice was far from steady.

"No. She is worthy, you are not. Her own galaxy flourished with her. Her remorse is genuine. Is yours?"

"You're not my superior. You're just another Second Order."

"You want to appeal to the Third Orders?" Messier looked up. "Don't you already know that outcome?"

"I can tell that everyone is against me."

"Don't try to get my sympathy. You pretended to reform yourself before."

Messier did not retreat an inch. The only sound was the subsiding wails issuing from Andromeda. At last Pi spoke. "I relinquish my command over the Milky Way and all claim to Andromeda."

"Peacefully, wholeheartedly?"

"Yes."

"Then stand, Andromeda."

After several seconds she put her hands on the floor and tried to get up. "I can't."

"Be strong. You need to set a good example for Pi. I'm given to know that this arrangement may not always be necessary. But for now, this is the only way."

*

Lifetimes passed.

*

A three-pointed star appeared. Oscar thought it must be a meteor. There seemed to be more every evening. Second Chance astronomers had chronicled the merger of the galaxies, commenting as the broadcast holos illustrated the slow-motion event.

The star was still coming toward him. Odd. It dimmed as it approached, though it was still bright enough to make afterimages when Oscar blinked. When it came to rest it was head high, small, and could be viewed without pain.

We need your help.

"Hardly looks like you need a tailor!" Oscar chuckled, then coughed.

This universe is still falling apart. It has to change direction or it will never come back together, never cycle again.

"Yes, the astronomers do talk about that. It's hardly my concern. What's trillions of years to me? I haven't many left." Oscar humored the voice in this crazy dream.

Remember.

Suddenly Oscar lost control of his body, spasming as though he were having an epileptic fit, but aware all the time. He was on the ground for minutes before it subsided. His mind swirled with new memories. How could that be?

I'm sorry. I forgot your limits, how little reality your kind can absorb.

Oscar used the door-frame to help his trembling body stay upright.

So far in this cycle, fear has held sway over love. We need help to attract the galaxies, to bring them back home.

"So just because our galaxy is joining another one, you think one man here can help you? Why not ask a gnat?"

You created a sentience of a higher order.

"These are not my memories. Me? Make that Pi monster? Ridiculous. If you were trying to make me feel guilty, you've failed."

True, that process was too costly.

The weight of memories of—maybe hundreds?—of lives was too much. He felt older than one person could ever be. Is this how insanity feels?

I handled this badly. My offer stands. When you have finished this life, you can take up the work if you choose. Tell me your answer then and I will bring you to us.

His head reverberated with people talking, too many! He sank to his knees.

Let this remind you.

A simple gold ring appeared and slipped on his finger. Yes, he located that memory. He had lost this in Pi's second attack. Vera!

Please help us. The star vanished with a soft pop.

Oscar shook his head, trying to clear it, but only succeeded in making himself dizzy. He staggered to the living room and rested in his favorite chair. After a few minutes he looked at his hand. The ring was still there.

His imagination filled with plans.

He died with a knowing smile on his lips.

*

"Do you want time to adjust, to rest from the death trauma?" A voice from everywhere and nowhere came to Oscar.

He replied, "It is an old wound, reopened. I've lived with the limp so long, it feels like my gait." The place was grey, indistinct, gradually growing an up and a down.

"We feel it may already be too late," the voice said.

Oscar said, "If there were a class of being beyond order, it would not say such a thing. Time is a construct of mind. We have the time we need, or can create it. We shall not imprison ourselves in what we built."

"It seems you allude to a solution that has escaped us so far."

"This much I do know, after the millions of years I've had to make mistakes and learn thereby. Separateness is an illusion. The Second Orders need to understand this. The First even have glimpses in ecstasy, whether in pairing, on the battlefield, or in contemplation of beauty. All the richness of all the individuals of any kind were implicit in the moments before the big bang. Alone, we are sterile, indistinct. We *need* contrast. We become what we are by relation to others, and becoming closer will make us more of what we are. In this paradox, truth."

Oscar found himself at the center of an Epidauran theater, bright beings hanging on his every word.

"So, in an obverse, looking-glass way, the ancient texts could be true all along. It wasn't that in the beginning, god created man and woman. No, rather, to bring the end, which is the only possible start at a new beginning, man and woman created god." There. That had the pull of truth.

An echo of ancient music rang through his mind, shaking him with its power. It was so subtle, but Oscar could feel, hear and see it. So could his audience, the acolytes among each of the many orders. They turned to the sound, like flowers soaking up the sunlight and Oscar smiled.

It would take many more lessons, many more symphonies, but he knew that unity would come at last, bringing with it fabulous energy and the bright burst of fresh creation.

***

Scott Davis's childhood imagination was fueled by the Tom Swift, Jr. serial novels he bought with allowance money at the local Zayers department store. Peter, his teenage friend introduced him to Asimov and high school English added Fahrenheit 451. His tastes haven't matured much since, though along the way he got a BA in Philosophy, an MBA, started a company he runs today and like Tom Swift and his Flying Lab, flies his own plane. His stories have appeared in Neo Opsis, 52 Stitches, *the* Terminal Earth *anthology and quite a few terminated markets.*

The Official

Fernando Salazar

He considered the entry papers one last time before presenting them to the waiting Official. Some he had carried a long way—one hundred light years in fact—others were new and had an alien feel, the fibers both moist and scratchy at the same time and the surface bedizened with strange, leaden characters. He strained his eyes to count the papers, his vision somewhat blurry in the odd light and strange atmosphere. Long as the journey from Earth might have been, the journeys from building to building and bureaucrat to bureaucrat seemed interminably longer. How long? Hours? Days? His sense of time had become no less blurred than his sense of sight. At last he had reached this hopefully final office. The walls of this place were peculiar; his weakened eyes could not place the textures and strange colors. Yet, at this point nothing concerned him but the office's lone desk and, behind it, the Official.

He paused, his glance lingering on one particular paper, the one that recorded by weight and volume his daily digestive "output" ever since his arrival, certified with signatures from three technicians. Such were the documentary requirements to secure the right to travel freely in this new place.

Yes, the familiar and the alien, the papers were all there. With trembling hands he arrayed them on the desk and now nothing was left but to await the uncertain stamp of the Official which, poised in mid-air, was clearly wavering between grudging acceptance and indignant denial. He adopted a demeanor of polite concern, hoping to best influence the Official, though he had no rational reason to suppose a specific configuration of human eyes, nose and mouth should impart any meaning whatsoever to a giant, trinocular, tentacled cephalopod—the Terran type closest in configuration to the Official. For its part, the Official was completely silent in its deliberations; the only evidence it betrayed of any awareness whatsoever was to now and then prod a paper with a tentacle.

As the noiseless delay continued, a feeling suddenly began to build within him, beyond his control almost—one part exhaustion, one part delirium, one part outrage, one part manic despair. Images surged through his mind and he struggled to hold back from acting on them: Screaming at top of his lungs; doing cartwheels; disrobing; and last—though it did him no credit—striking the Official with a stick. He paused and pondered; would such an action have any effect on the Official's gelatinous exterior? He had no idea, but at that moment he was sure the satisfaction of the act would be immense.

Then the Official spoke and he sighed in relief, composing himself to listen.

"Again ... me telling please why you must living here are to be?"

The auto-translator somewhat mangled the word order, but the sense of the Official's question was clear. He phrased his response slowly so the translator would have maximum accuracy.

"I am an expert in the automation of business activities. I have come at the invitation of your government, and in the hope of greater cooperation between our species, to use my expertise for your benefit."

The Official slowly turned its stamp over and over between its tentacled "fingers." It then asked a further question.

"Benefit ... these precisely being are?"

The answer came quickly—too quickly. "The elimination of paper, for one. With our devices, all your information and decisions can be captured as patterns of energy, all stored in a tiny device the size of your—the size of *my* fist. No more paper! Imagine ... the efficiency .... "

He stopped talking as the Official slowly lowered the stamp. His gaze followed one stalked eye as it swiveled to the left, another eye as it swiveled right, and then a third eye as it swiveled all about. Though he couldn't be certain—maybe it was the rhythmic way the eye stalks waved—he thought the three separate eyes all were charged with affectionate longing. He stepped back to better view what the Official was gazing at so intently.

It was paper. What he had first taken for walls really was paper: A cocoon of paper, a fortress of paper, leaved, folded and bound ramparts of paper. As he squinted his eyes in the hazy alien light, he saw papers bound with dull purple strings, faded green ribbons, burnt-orange folders. He saw papers dense with miniscule type, papers with diagrams in abstruse geometry, papers with clever adhesive annotations, and with annotation on annotation, papers flimsy as silk, papers stout as leather, papers stamped with seals, some like bold mandalas, some like proud insignias, and still others like blunt wounds and bruises. And now the paper smell came to him, a single aroma—old and strong—that melded the multifarious races of forms, depositions, records, leases, deeds, behests, certificates and permissions into a unified defensive corps that would resist any assault to the last leaf.

As he turned back he saw the Official take up a new stamp. After an instant's pause the Official rained stamping hammer blows on his application, each blow landing with a jaunty click of the inking mechanism and leaving behind a pale brown lightning bolt of negativity. Then the auto-translator spoke:

"Earthman—Request denied. Nice day having instance of."

***

*A technology executive for a global company, **Fernando Salazar** struggles to fit too many outside interests—like Aikido, history, wine, amateur theatrics and writing—into too little free time. He makes his long-term home in Arlington, Mass., with wife Kim and daughters Alex and Morgan. As of this writing Fernando is in the midst of a 2 year assignment in India, living and working in the city of Pune; "The Official" is only one of a number of stories that have come from his experiences in this ancient and complex culture. Fernando writes about expatriate life, travel, technology and more at his blog, fjsalazar.com.*

Diversity

LJ Cohen

Varna bit back the urge to click her tongue in distress as she studied her tall, barrel-chested boss. Ambassador Berwick's voice, so well suited to vid broadcasts and important speeches to even more important people, felt far too large for her small cubicle. She struggled to keep her throat relaxed and her overvoice silent.

"Your participation is essentially a formality," he said, leaning over her desk and smiling.

Despite her discomfort at being in his spotlight, it was hard not to smile back. Berwick had a charm that came across as both well-practiced and genuine, almost childlike in its enthusiasm.

"You're not technically part of the diplomatic team and the actual negotiations will take place after the welcoming ceremony. So, what do you think?" he asked.

She clasped her hands under the desk to keep from fidgeting. Varna had worked at the Embassy long enough to know it didn't really matter what she thought. His direct presence here made her assignment to the mission merely seem like a request instead of genetic expediency.

What did she think? Varna clamped her teeth down. After a lifetime of struggling to pass in Human society, she thought this was a massive mistake. But you didn't just say that to Earth's most high-ranking inter-planetary Ambassador. Hell, Berwick probably spoke more of her grandparents' native Tuvlun than she did, and he didn't even have the properly shaped palate. She didn't realize she was tapping the tip of her tongue against the high arch of her mouth until the hollow echo of her anxiety filled the room. She snapped her mouth closed before the clicking could annoy him.

"What about my assignments?" She glanced across the piles of perma-paper scattered across her desk.

Berwick raised the bushy eyebrows that framed his steel gray eyes.

Varna's ears thrummed. What a stupid question, but she had to find a way out of this. She wasn't really Tuv, no matter what a gene-scan might show. Her grandparents had turned their backs on their native culture in the clearest way they knew how: they raised their only son—her father—to pursue some bizarre version of a Human life in Tuv skin. As far as she knew, the few other Tuv refugees on Earth had done the same. She shook her head. How much harder it must have been for that first generation. At least she could pass, even if most of the time, she felt like she failed at being either Tuv or Human.

"You've been released from Human Resources until further notice."

She shook her head at his unintended irony and swallowed the braying laugh that always betrayed her Tuv heritage. Tall for an Earth woman, taller even than Berwick, most of Varna's differences remained internal, including the double set of vocal cords that let her voice call out tones her mother complained sounded like a cross between an owl and a cat in heat.

"I'm looking forward to working with you, Varna," Berwick said, glancing at the nameplate on her desk, trying to puzzle out the pronunciation of her last name. She didn't know why she bothered to hold onto that one vestige of her heritage. Everyone mangled it anyway.

"Just use Vee. It's easier than the full formal version." Her nervous laugh filled the small work cubicle. It rang overly loud to her sensitive ears, but it was the best she could do, despite years of speech therapy and coaching. "Even I have trouble sometimes." Her grandfather's lessons echoed in her memory: *Put others at ease. Don't call attention to yourself. Fit in. Your job is to dress, walk, and speak like an ordinary Human.*

"So how do you pronounce it?" Berwick leaned forward, his eyebrows raised in an expression of curiosity.

Was he really interested? Or did he just need to know she had enough Tuv in her genome to fulfill the Tuvlun envoy's demands? She would have to pay attention to the more subtle tonalities in his voice to tell the difference between Berwick-the-person and Berwick-the-Ambassador. Her Tuvlun senses were very out of practice.

"I'm afraid you don't have the range to hear it exactly the way a Tuv might, sir. This is as close as I can get." She took a breath and let air vibrate the small, thin vocal cords she worked so hard to silence. Her family name emerged as something partly spoken, partly sung, and partly pure vibration she could feel against the sensitive membrane in her ears.

Berwick winced and took a step back.

Heat rushed to Varna's face in a completely Human response to embarrassment. "I'm so sorry, Ambassador!"

He put his hands up and shook his head. "No, not at all. The attaché warned me we would all need auditory filters for the formal meetings. I just didn't think I would need them quite yet."

Looking down at her cluttered desk, she wondered how she could possibly escape. She was no diplomat. Unlike her wandering fore-bearers, Varna had barely even left the solar system, and her grandparents, native Tuvlun stranded on Earth, rarely spoke about their home. "Sir, I really think …"

"That you're not the woman for the job? That you'll cause a diplomatic incident? That we should choose someone else?"

She dropped her gaze to the floor. Yes, yes, and yes. To all of the above.

"Your supervisors think very highly of you, you know."

Sure. That and a trans-pass could get her to the moon and back. She lifted her eyes to his face again and swallowed past the lump in her overly long throat. "There are others a lot more qualified. Sir."

He sat at the edge of her desk and leaned in. "So my advisers tell me."

Varna hadn't expected that. Her face heated again and the blood beat against the inner membranes of her ears like the pounding of drums.

"The Tuv will only meet with us if the delegation contains someone who can claim Tuvlun heritage. Fortunately for us, you were already working in my Embassy, with full security clearance and the freedom to accompany me in the time window we have." He smiled. "Besides, I have a feeling about you, Varna."

Not that it mattered, but she tried one more time. "Look, I have no idea what I'm doing. I'm no diplomat. I'm an assistant to an assistant …"

He waved down her objections. "None of us ever do," he said, a far-away look on his face.

Berwick's vulnerability surprised her, though it could just be a diplomatic maneuver—something to put her at ease. Should she tell him her grandparents got practically thrown out of the Tuv trade guild and off-planet?

"Don't worry, my attaché will get you up to speed. Welcome aboard." He gave her a slight bow and left her office without shaking her hand. She didn't know if that meant anything.

*

They might as well have been on any in-system transport with its small and featureless rooms, and the bland, institutional food. No sense of movement accompanied the terrible dislocation Varna felt. For the most part, she tried to keep to herself in her tiny cabin except for the mandatory meetings and daily briefings.

Slouching low in her chair in the conference room, she listened as the ranking general complained about the newly established Tuv trading base so close to Earth's only major nexus point. Berwick's second-in-command insisted the placement simply allowed for a face-to-face meeting and that the Tuv didn't pose any military threat.

Besides, allying with the Tuv promised to give Earth access to a whole series of new nexus points. That alone, the diplomats argued, made the risk worth it since the Tuv had resisted every offer to trade until now. The same set of facts made the general and his small military contingent twitchy.

Each side presented its best-and-worst-case scenarios, then everyone in the cramped room looked at her as if she had some insider knowledge of the Tuv grand plan. Varna wanted to shrink her too-tall body, silence her too-resonant voice, and hide in her cabin until it was all over.

Berwick barely said more than a few words to her. He had his own team of advisers and seemed to be frowning in concentration whenever she saw him.

She knew it probably irritated the rest of the mission the way it had always irritated her mother, but Varna spent a lot of time humming deep in her throat to try and soothe her nerves. It wasn't easy overriding a childhood where she was taught to hide all outward evidence of her Tuv roots. In a strange way, she felt like she was betraying her grandparents.

Every possible moment, she poured over the ceremony wording to make sense not only of her role, but of the whole formal presentation. Parts of it felt like a debate, other parts like a wedding. The exchange of trade agreements seemed simple, but the heart of the ceremony included the offering of official gifts. The diplomats argued every day over what they should present to the Tuv.

They had also prepared a short speech for her to give in Standard and in Tuvlun. Many of the Tuv words didn't make a whole lot of sense even when she had the computer take its best shot at translation. Her grandparents had been the last Tuv to seek asylum on Earth. The language database had to be woefully out of date.

Only a brief announcement warned them they'd docked before the external ports turned transparent again. The nexus point wasn't all that impressive to look at. A series of gantries and scaffolding floated at odd angles to one another, sprouting from a dot in space that Varna's eye skipped over, no matter how hard she tried to look at it. The Tuv had the largest nexus network in this part of the galaxy and they were suddenly willing to share it with Earth. No wonder the Embassy jumped at the opportunity.

Varna stared out at the field of stars beyond the nexus, but she had no way of knowing which was her adopted sun and which might have been her Grandparents' long lost home star.

"What am I doing here?" she asked.

"Remarkable, isn't it?"

Varna yelped in surprise, her overvoice ringing the room. Ambassador Berwick winced and covered his ears.

"I'm so sorry, sir," she said.

"My fault. I didn't mean to startle you." He rubbed at his temples.

After the flurry of activity on their way to the rendezvous, it seemed strange seeing him in a quiet moment and without several men and women at his side. At least one from the diplomatic team and one from the military group had flanked him at all times, like an angel and devil on his shoulders. She wondered which was which.

He frowned, patting his pockets. "Here they are." He drew out a set of tiny filters. "We haven't had a chance to fully field-test them. Shall we?"

She looked at him, drawing her eyebrows together as he fitted them to his ears.

"Go on. Say something in Tuvlun."

She took a deep breath and recited one of the lines from her script, watching the Ambassador's face carefully, but he didn't react.

"Excellent," he said, nodding.

Well, at least she could get through her speech without sending her own delegation screaming out of the ceremony.

"For what it's worth, I appreciate your part in this."

He appeared as confident as ever, but his voice had a ringing overtone that betrayed his nerves. She didn't think she would have noticed before spending hours and hours retraining her ears with the Tuvlun language simulators. "Sir?" But he had gone before she had a chance to say anything else.

*

The next time she saw the Ambassador, he stood, dressed in formal gray and silver, in the entry to the large chamber where the Tuv delegation had created a meeting hall. Berwick paused at the edge of the cold, white room, its floor bare but for the red and gold lights that winked in the shape of a curved runway leading to where their Tuv counterparts stood. The rest of the Earth delegation waited at the perimeter, military honor guard and the Ambassador's staff alike. She kept her eyes on Berwick. What was he waiting for? Varna started humming, but cut off the buzzing sound at a shake of his head, wishing she had something to do with her hands.

The room fell silent. Even the Earth delegation stood completely motionless. Varna still had not looked up from her study of the floor. What if they wanted someone more obviously Tuv? From what she'd been able to piece together from childhood, her grandparents had been permanently exiled from their homeworld. She never knew why. What if their failure reflected on her? Her spindly arms hung at her sides, wrists poking out from the sleeves. She clicked her tongue rapidly against the roof of her mouth. This was such a mistake.

Berwick met her eyes and smiled. He had such a large presence it seemed wrong that she stood taller than he did. When he finally gave her a nod, she stumbled forward on wobbly legs. He walked beside and slightly behind her, holding the box containing the gifts the staff had finally agreed to offer. She wasn't even sure what had ended up in the container. The Ambassador should be the one in front, not her. She struggled not to glance back at him and focused on her feet and on not tripping along the way to the dais.

Forcing her head up, she nearly gasped aloud at her first good look at the waiting delegation. The Tuv representative stepped forward from a group of five others. He looked like her grandfather must have before the years on Earth had aged him and stooped his body. Standing nearly seven feet tall, with a long neck and thin oval face, he towered over even her. His round eyes, nearly black, almost all pupil, were as impossible to read as her grandparents' and her father's had been. Dark green robes flowed over a black form-fitting bodysuit that accentuated his lean limbs. She wondered if that's what she looked like to her Human friends and co-workers—a walking, talking scarecrow.

"Daughter of Tuv, be welcome here. I am the Speaker." She recognized the words from her studying. His voice rumbled through her. Her grandmother's voice had sounded like that and Varna realized how flat, how empty Human voices seemed in comparison. The Speaker turned to Ambassador Berwick and folded his lanky torso into a bow. "She is well chosen." His Standard rang through the room in multiple octaves simultaneously, but all the members of their delegation had filters in place. At least no one winced.

The Speaker clasped his arms together and waited. A long silence fell. Now what? Varna had an almost irresistible urge to say something, say anything to fill the void, but she forced herself to be still. The Speaker studied her for several uncomfortable moments before unlacing and relacing his fingers.

The silence stretched out until she practically vibrated with tension. Her hands shook. He was supposed to say something. This was not what she had practiced. Sweat trickled down her back and she glanced back at the Ambassador. He nodded, his face composed. A soft hum rose from the Tuv side of the room. It resonated against her thin second ear drum and she shivered with the collision of the familiar and the strange. She wiped her palms against the soft material of her formal robes.

Just a formality. Just a formality. She looped the Ambassador's words over and over in her head in a calming mantra.

A young Tuv girl stepped forward from behind the Speaker, holding a smooth, seamless white box. Varna let her shoulders relax. This had to be the exchange of official gifts. They were back on the script. The girl stroked the box with the slender fingers of her right hand. All the fingers measured the same length, even the thumb. Varna looked down at her own hands, the fingers almost like her mother's. Her own thumbs seemed impossibly squat and clumsy next to the girl's.

The box unfolded itself, revealing four small, triangular compartments, each filled with a glass vial. Perfume? Something to drink? What was she supposed to do?

The girl set the open box on a waiting table and drew out one of the vials. The liquid inside swirled a dark purple that was nearly black. "Please, you will hold?" she asked, her Standard awkward and halting. Varna could sense Berwick somewhere behind her. Surely he would intervene if this were dangerous.

Varna reached out and took the vial in her right hand. The crystal caught the light and splashed rainbows against the chamber walls.

The girl reached out and gripped Varna's left forearm. She plucked the stopper from the bottle with her other hand and squeezed a single drop of fluid over their crossed wrists. A shadow the color of dusk rose between them. Varna tried to step back. The girl hissed a warning she couldn't translate and gripped even tighter.

"A gift to awaken Tuv senses," the Speaker said, first in Standard, then in Tuvlun.

Varna relaxed and peered into the darkness. Sheets of color burst into her vision. She blinked furiously, trying to clear her eyes, but the brightness bloomed everywhere, creating her own personal aurora borealis. The room came back into view and the light show faded. The girl nodded, placed the stopper back in the bottle and plucked it from Varna's hand, sliding it back into the box. She chose a second vial. Red liquid shimmered inside.

Varna took a deep breath and nodded as one drop hung from the stopper. It slowly sheeted off to splash on their skin. A humming started at her feet. Her bones thrummed with it and her entire body vibrated. The hairs on her arms fanned out. In the distance, she heard what sounded like tolling bells, one peal overlapping with another and another until the whole room rang. The inside of her mind formed a cathedral. Varna's breathing sped up. Tears welled up in her eyes when the last of the echoes faded away.

She barely felt the girl taking the red vial and giving her another. This one glowed a deep night sky blue. Scents she didn't even have words for triggered memories long locked inside. Her father's cologne brought his face into focus. He held her hand with his, impossibly long fingers curled entirely around her small, stunted ones. "When will my fingers grow right, Daddy?" she asked. Other scents crowded out his answer. She smelled the special steamed bread from her childhood, pungent with a spice her grandmother could never replicate on Earth after her small store from home ran out.

Tastes bloomed on her tongue: The first time she tried chocolate and gagged on the bitterness. The odd combinations of sweet and spicy she always craved. Each taste burned with a color in her mind, each color rang with a clear tone. Her body felt distant, impossibly large and microscopic at the same time. She fell into the heart of a nexus point, except it blazed with light and swelled larger and larger as she got closer to it.

The bright crash of breaking glass brought time and space rushing back. Varna swayed on trembling legs, her hands empty. Cerulean liquid from the dropped vial pooled at her feet. She stared into a distorted mirror of herself. The young Tuv woman looked back. "What … how … " She wasn't sure what language spilled out. It didn't matter. The words rolled around her mouth. They had shape and texture. She could taste their meaning.

She blinked her blurred vision clear, looked up into the Speaker's deep eyes, and dropped into a well of sadness, of patience measured across lifetimes and by the slow shift of constellations across silent space. He reached his free hand out toward her, hesitantly, the arc of its movement asking for permission, for forgiveness.

Images of her grandparents filled her mind with memories clearer than her Earth-dulled senses had ever captured. Her very Human eyes filled with tears. "Thank you for this gift," Varna said.

The Tuv words she used felt right, full of nuance that any Standard form of gratitude would have lacked.

"It is your birthright, daughter of Tuv, too long delayed," the Speaker said. Again, the Tuvlun echoed with additional meanings. Guilt and regret hummed in the air like the lowest string of a harp. Her grandparents were the ones exiled, the ones who broke faith with their own people. What would he have to be guilty about?

Ambassador Berwick fidgeted behind her. The whisper of his clothing rasped like sandpaper against her ears. The entire delegation shifted in growing restlessness. Before she could take the box from him and offer their gifts in turn, the Tuv girl turned to the Speaker. At his nod, she snatched up a sliver of glass from the floor at her feet. It winked in her fingers. Varna stared without moving as the girl grabbed her hand again in an unshakeable grip, the sharp glass trapped between them, cutting into both their palms.

Varna gasped. Pale blood, Tuv and partly Tuv, seeped from their joined hands for a moment before the pain blossomed. It was a shared pain. And out of it emerged a third language—not Standard, not Tuvlun, but something deeper than either could have been alone.

The girl reached for the fourth vial and collected a single drop of their mingled blood. A silence larger and colder than space blanketed the room. The blood pounded in her head. Distant shouts reminded her she wasn't alone. She looked up and a ring of security men pressed too close, assembling a cordon around the Ambassador. She could taste their fear, their desire for weapons locked on the ship under diplomatic seal.

"The sharing is complete," the girl said, capping the vial, her words limned with fatigue and triumph.

Ambassador Berwick stood, the sealed box still in his hands. Tension vibrated across his shoulders. "We have come here in the spirit of peace, Speaker." His words purpled with anxiety and reproach. He did not meet Varna's desperate gaze.

"I swear, she has not been harmed," the Speaker said, meeting Berwick's gaze with his own.

Berwick turned his head to look at Varna. She nodded. It was the truth. The small cut would heal cleanly.

The Ambassador ordered the Earth security to stand down. Practiced discipline dimmed their burnt-orange aura as they took parade-rest positions by the chamber door, leaving her and the Tuv girl isolated in the center of the room. The girl bowed and retreated with the rest of the Tuv delegation, until only the Speaker remained.

He studied the Ambassador. "Thank you," the Speaker said. "The nexus maps are downloaded into your ship's mainframe."

Berwick frowned, his thick eyebrows pulling together. The waiting delegation relaxed in a symphony of sighs and rustling fabric.

"This gift honors us all," the Speaker said. Varna tasted his anguish, sharp and pungent on her tongue.

"I don't understand," she whispered.

"You will," the Speaker answered. "Your grandparents did."

"My grandparents?"

The Speaker smiled and bowed to her. "They have returned to us in you."

Something eased in the back of her throat. "They weren't outcasts?"

"No. Never." The truth in his voice filled the room with the scent of baking bread and the lost spices her grandmother had mourned. "They are honored for their choice, as you will be."

Her cut palm tingled where her strange, confused DNA had mixed with that of the Tuv girl, creating something new, something alive with possibility that Varna had no name for in either language.

"Now do you understand?"

When she exhaled, her breath hummed like the buzz of late summer bees. She closed her eyes. "Yes," she whispered. Her grandfather had pushed his son to mimic the culture around him to the point where he couldn't even speak passable Tuvlun. It was never out of shame, but out of duty. Out of sadness. Out of love. So that someday, his granddaughter could return, bringing something new to their people.

She glanced back at Ambassador Berwick still clutching the delegation's official gifts, confusion and jubilation competing for his expression. "Was it ... is it worth the cost?" she asked, her voice cracking.

The Speaker opened his palms and his fingers spread out like the spokes of a wheel. "We will not know for many turns, child."

She looked down at her own too human fists. "Why?"

"It has been our way since our fore-bearers touched the stars."

"You ask too much," she said, her heart breaking for her grandparents' sacrifice.

"We ask for your forgiveness."

The room sang with silence. Varna unclenched her hands. The glass splinter tumbled to the floor. "Now what?"

"Daughter of two worlds, you will always have a place of honor here, if you choose to stay." The Speaker took a step closer.

Berwick's indrawn breath was as loud as a shout. "She is a citizen of Earth, under the protection of the embassy."

She glanced between the two representatives, one Human, the other Tuv, feeling pulled between them. "Do all of us return? Or are some always lost, children of neither world?"

The Speaker averted his face. "We try to be worthy of their sacrifice. And yours."

"You ask too much," she said again, softly, her heart aching for those scattered sisters and brothers.

"The choice is yours," Berwick whispered, placing a gentle hand on her shoulder.

Both men waited as Varna listened to the mixed blood sing in her veins.

***

Lisa Janice (LJ) Cohen is a poet and novelist, blogger, local food enthusiast, Doctor Who fan, and relentless optimist. LJ lives just outside of Boston with her husband, teenage sons, two dogs (only one of which actually ever listens to her) and the occasional international student. Her debut novel, The Between *is available in all the usual places. You can connect with LJ via her blog: http://ljcbluemuse.blogspot.com and her website: http://www.ljcohen.net.*

Tear Apart Worlds

Chris Howard

Fundra put the thunderbird to sleep, her tips pressing the two-meter wings into hundred-fold angles. Bird bone spines and feathers fused into layers, the whole animal sliding paper thin and easily rolled into her community pocket. She made a gesture of sixteen tips because she felt sad, because she had fallen in love with the bird's eyes, glassy dark and wise.

Under the shade of fanning citrus orchards she could just see Bilk's house across Jihmeer Warless Meadow in the guest human settlement, ovals of light and smeared reflection along a tube that stuck out of one end of the Gib-Letton family residence. She thought it fun that Bilk called his piece of the house his "wing."

"Not like a thunderbird has wings?" she had asked him, and played the memory again.

Fundra had arrayed eleven tips like one raised eyebrow and Bilk had nodded. "Just like them. A limb off the main structure." He held out his muscular arms, hands dancer straight, fingers rigid. He smiled. "An arm, a leg will work well for the word, but a wing has a beauty that humans don't possess. You gave us the maps and tools to jump the gaps between stars. Since the beginning we've crossed worlds with our legs, and built them with our hands. But to soar over them without machinery? We do not have the grace, the beauty of a bird. We can only dream of having wings."

Ugliness was a funny subject with humans. They rarely looked anywhere but inside themselves for it. Ugliness and sorrow—so intimate for humankind. Fundra had made a sound like a laugh, a choppy twist of her voice that she'd learned to perform when she was with her fellow otherworld colonists. Then she had pointed to Bilk's wing of the house. "And you sleep in a wing?"

"Normally." He'd mimicked her laugh, sounding not quite human. "I dream when I sleep. Sometimes of wings. But more often of fins and swimming quick beneath the sea. Or I dream of a long time ago when I kicked under the waves of Chaleur Bay with my sister Nikola."

Fundra turned away from the memory, drifting home in the waves, and thought about tomorrow, when she would spend more time with Bilk, the human boy who had ugly and sorrow inside with his beauty and love of growth, who spent his sleeping time with shadows of himself running from old worlds, building new ones and flying over them, all in the wing of his house.

Unanchored to the sea floor, she fanned out and flowed with the currents, becoming a part of the water around her, chemically so much like her origin world so far away—but so much more than that world because she had grown into her forty-eight tips here on the planet her kind had opened to the humans. And, as if returning the gift, they'd called it Thetis. This world Thetis, where she had learned enough to understand the folding rules and how to tip the shapes of things like thunderbirds—things from Bilk's own mind and memories—into this world with them. Even with forty-eight, she wasn't allowed to make whole worlds yet—not without supervision.

Nothing slowed Fundra down when the sun rose over the great oceans of Thetis, when she could return to Bilk's house without alarming anyone, when the humans would wake and rub their beautiful eyes. She pulsed in the strength of the shore's currents, surfacing near the settlement at the end of the beach that wrapped one side of the Warless Meadow.

The Gib-Lettons were up and making coffee when Fundra used two tips—a simple move—to coil long cables of her body into a hard lump she used to knock on the front door. Humans were informal—at least these were. Gustav, Bilk's father, called out, "Door's not locked," and she slid through the opening, fanning out in the tiled area they called a "dinette." Jovita swung around the counter with a mug of hot coffee, lifting it a little in offering. Fundra declined, but continued staring. Bilk's mother had eyes rich and green like chlorophylled shallows.

Inside the Gib-Lettons' house, Fundra pulled together most of her body, long tendrils weaving into thick globs that hung over chairs, rolled halfway up the stairs, draped like heavy cloth over the banister, but she kept her senses focused on the kitchen and the pungent citrus smell—a good smell, she had determined.

Leaning over the bundles at the foot of the stairs, Jovita shouted, "Bilk, get up. Fundra's here."

"Lemons" said Gustav, catching Fundra's interest in the citrus smell. Then he went on sipping his coffee, spinning slowly inside a cylinder of infoscreens, keeping just enough focus on his surroundings to know that he had an audience. "The Cansons and us have a fine citrus crop going this season. The Huberys, alas, are still catching up."

"Have you eaten? You're early." Bilk stood at the top of the stairs, yawning, rubbing one eye with a fist.

"Every moment I'm in the water, and I have no need of early. Oceans do not sleep, my friend Bilk." Fundra streamed rows of fluid appendages toward the open front door. "We have little need for early or late, spending all our time looking for the answer. Is the answer to humanity open in the way you delight in things that grow? Lemons? Does it hide in the ways you express sorrow? Or is there something more?" Humans were like sharp little tidal forces, each one an ocean in the grasp of a strong moon, drawing up and awake for a short time, then falling asleep, waking, sleeping, spending their entire lives tied to the cycle. It was one of the first interesting facts she'd learned about her world guests. The second had been that they had named the colonized world after a mythical sea deity—and how lovely of them.

Realizing he wasn't dressed in much, Bilk tugged at his shirt, and back-stepped to his room to get ready for their day of exploration. He threw on his drysuit, jumped the bundles of Fundra at the bottom of the stairs, and raced for the front door with a wave at his parents. Thetis was cleared of most human threats by Fundra's family of oceanfarers. And any bad things that remained were land-based. "The waters are clear," as Fundra's mother Niyallor had said when the humans arrived.

Down at the shore, Bilk slid the suit's seams closed to his throat, and bayonetted his helmet seal, mimicking—with his tongue behind his teeth—the hard click the pressure locks made. He looked up at Fundra. "All set?"

"Are you asking if I have reconfigured for a different environment in the last few moments? I am ready to journey, if that's what you mean."

"Don't want to jinx anything." Bilk wagged finger, and a worried look pressed itself into his features. "I have to ask the check-off question." Bilk waved away the conversation and started a new one, pointing over the sea. "Dawn is here. I have until dusk to make the most of the day. Where shall we go, Fundra?"

"Down is always good. I usually advise that to start out."

"You usually? You're a body of water. When *don't* you think down is good?"

"Thunderbirds have been on my mind lately."

"And you can now advise a course of *up* to start out instead of down? Or how about both, hopping up and down like a kangaroo?"

"Kangaroos do not interest me in the same way the thunderbird does."

"Ever hear of the prehistoric vampire kangaroo—tales of the monstrous, the blood-thirsty, the pouched predator, fangaroo?" Bilk strolled into the foam and rolling waves, bending to get his fingers wet. He looked over at her, smiled. "They're silly—sillier than a thunderbird by far."

Surf crashed against Fundra's fluid bulk, and she flowed with it, lapping up the beach, ten meter nerve strands and paddles drawn into the curl of the next wave. "My ancestor Jelishild would have been able to create a fangaroo if she wanted. She could create anything. She grew to one hundred and fourteen tips, and could topple and twist and turn whole galaxies on edge. Her volume spanned a thousand planets, and she tip-built the plumbing to a thousand unflowing galactic spaces. You and I are here on

Thetis because Jelishild tipped here before us."

"Tipped a world?" Bilk spread his fingers in a flowing gesture. "How do you build a world-path? How do you chart the paths to stars and worlds? So many out there. How do you even know which stars to choose?"

"How do you know this is the right place to enter the sea?" Fundra twirled a few tips into a pointing finger, and wagged it along the beach. "Because you have been here before, Bilk. Because you have made the path through the dunes to this point on the shore. Finding a new and whole breathable world is not easy. It's not impossible, but it's also not productive. Jelishild's way—and now ours—is to create the worlds, form them with her power, flow over their surfaces, supply the life and wealth, and then tread the path from other worlds a few times to make it clear and mappable by others—our own kind, and our guests."

Excited by the thought of some of Fundra's kind—the over-hundred-tipped among them—building their own worlds, Bilk lunged forward, and went under the waves, determined to explore more of this one, Fundra smoothing out around him in long threaded currents that curled and pulsed.

Tears started up as soon as Bilk hit thirty-one meters, soft salt splattering the inside of his face mask. He tried to stop them, tried to shove the safety checklist from his mind, and he sucked in a deep breath over shuddering rows of sorrow. He was still sobbing at sixty meters.

"Bilk?" Fundra ran three tips along the back of his suit, curling at his shoulders, sent the last to coil over his helmet and tap on the face mask.

"I looked down at my depth meter right at thirty-one. Sorry." Bilk's voice came back distant, choppy with pain. "I thought I'd cried it all out a long time ago. My twin, my sister, died at thirty-one meters. When we lived on Chaleur Bay—on Earth. We moved to Florida, then to Coquimbo in Chile." He waved a thick gloved finger at the surrounding dark blue. "We are here not because Jelishild made the path, but because I lost my sister. My parents had to get away from everything. They couldn't bear to be in the same world that killed her."

Running tears slid down the inside of his face mask, puddling in the voice instruments. Bilk blinked to clear his vision, throwing one arm out reflexively, cupping the water and pulling at it to find his direction. He heard Nikola's voice—his sister speaking, and then a tingle up his neck. He felt someone breathing the same air. Then he lost touch with the world. It slipped away from him.

"Do not move." Fundra went into an emergency mothering curl, surrounding Bilk in a sphere of surface pressure space, and he drifted into a roll, landing on his back, his helmet thumping hard on an artificial floor.

A web of finger-thin appendages shot out and spun off Bilk's shoulder and throat cuffs. The helmet sagged back and skidded away, and Fundra's gentle fingers slipped around his neck and head to hold him up.

"Wait, Bilk. Do not leave this world yet." Fundra gave him a few tugs. "Come back to me. Look at me." Then panic slipped into her voice as she watched a fresh flow of tears start. "No, Bilk. Do not create new worlds here. I will not be able to contain them. You must hold on to your tears."

A shudder ran through Bilk, and he focused, swiveled his gaze to Fundra's face, a mass of sensory knobs and wave flaps and chemoanalyst panels. She was beautiful and he smiled as she lifted one of his tears away with a single tip, gently, a benign goddess handling someone's soul. The little sphere of saline wobbled and Bilk felt her fear.

"You are too late, my friend." Fundra spread seven tips for sorrow.

*

They were all there—and all worried: Bilk's mother and father, two of the human colony reps, Tenna Serice, Greg Kintreias, and the whole Hubery family, who were just really nosy and had a mild rivalry going with the Gib-Lettons.

"Gone for two days?" Serice, the col-rep, used the tip of her shoe to make an S in the sand at her feet. "We contacted Home, but it'll be another couple days before we get an answer back. In the meantime ..." Her voice trailed off with the hope that a good idea would appear before she had to take the next breath.

"They sent us this." Bilk's father, Gustav, held up a thin, metallic-looking elliptical shape with feathered edges and four rows of irregular spines. He got a shaking head from Kintreias, who had already run the thing through the labs.

Bilk's mother, Jovita, pulled it from his hands, holding it up to the light. "No idea how to open it."

"Do you read it?" said one of the Huberys, mildly irritated that the Gib-Lettons had received something they hadn't.

"It looks like it needs to be opened or turned on." Jovita handed it back to Gustav, sighing. "Bilk would know what to do with it. We're assuming it's a message, something to be read, or to interact with."

Kintreias was chewing his lip, then stopped to say, "Most of their tech requires a minimum of twenty-eight tips—something all their children have grown into." He chewed a little more, then added, "Twenty-eight's the minimum just to read the labels, just to find out what something is. Their simplest toys require the twenty-eight. We've analyzed thousands of their tools and devices with up to sixty tip requirements, recorded molecular structures and patterning, and tried to match particle signatures. We've seen nothing like this. It could be a simple letter. It could be payment for losing your son." He scratched his head. "We have no idea."

The surface of the sea before them flattened and then heaved with eight giant watery shapes, tendrils swinging into the air. Three more of Fundra's kind seeped up through the sand behind the humans, curling and flattening out so they wouldn't tower over them and frighten them. Oceans in their smallest forms were still terrifyingly large.

Fundra's father was in the center of the group, looking angry to Jovita's eye. But he didn't sound angry, his voice smooth, soft surf over level sand. "Jovita and Gustav, welcome." He swung forty transparent tendrils into a fan shape across the beach with a graceful stem that pointed at the metallic thing in Gustav's hands. "I am glad you have received and accepted our request for a formal meeting." He indicated the two human colony reps, made a curling motion with half his body, perhaps attempting a bow. "And you have gathered advisors and friends."

Jovita stepped forward, one hand gripping Gustav's shoulder hard. She pulled in a breath, let it out to put some calm in her voice. "What can you tell us of our son—and Fundra?"

"A confession first. We were just speaking among ourselves of confessions and coincidence and loss. We have lost our daughter Fundra and you have lost your son Bilk. It is no coincidence that they were together to share a day, and together they are lost. We are searching, and we must confess that we have found no trace of Fundra in this world. She is..." He spent a few seconds searching for a word. "Gone."

Gustav looked past the gathering at the horizon. "And Bilk is with her."

"You are not equipped ..." Fundra's father stammered in translation, mixing in choppy notes and long curling R sounds.

"We do not mean to offend," said another of Fundra's kind from behind the humans.

"We blame my daughter. She is an answer gatherer—trained to find the answer of your kind, but she is also ..."

They didn't find out what Fundra also was. Fundra's father sounded unsure. "She has perhaps grown into another twelve tips, giving her enough to create and visit another world. Perhaps she pushed too hard for the answer."

Gustav stepped forward, holding the metallic device in both hands, shaking. "I don't understand. She has taken Bilk with her? Can they come back to this one?"

Just the wind over the waves for an answer.

*

"You said it's too late." Bilk laughed, scooping the water past his body. "In what way is it too late?"

"Your mother will be upset with you."

Bilk frowned. "And not my father?"

"He is concerned with lemons," she said as if this made perfect sense.

"And you think citrus fruit will ease his mind?" He laughed again.

"At least it is clear to me that he will understand growth." Fundra lifted long strands of her own body and slipped under him, surrounding and protecting him, closing as if preparing to pull him out of the life inside his own tear.

Bilk waved her off. "I'm not ready to leave."

He spun, taking it all in. How could he leave? A single teardrop contained all this.

The world around Bilk was thick like the sea but full of winged creatures soaring—some like thunderbirds that flew in fluid. He bent his body and headed straight down, the darker, the deeper, the scarier the better. He just knew it. And Fundra was there with him, racing alongside, keeping pace in her between-the-water frictionless form.

Bilk looked over his shoulder and watched the last of the tears slide off his face, tiny flashes of bright silver skipping end over end into his turbulent wake. He was on his way back to the shallows when he noticed he wasn't wearing his helmet—and then with some choking shock—that he didn't seem to need it. The water was inside his lungs ... if he still had lungs here. This was a different world. He was different. And like a dream in which the most absurd things can slip by without question, Bilk forgot about possibilities and breathing devices, waving playfully at Fundra and laughing.

His drysuit slipped away, imaginary here, dissolving in the sea. He was soaring in a sleek new body, silver bright arms and cupping transparent fingers catching the water and moving it under him. And he felt ... infinite and multiple and connected to every reflection of himself the sea showed him. He felt the memory well in every molecule made of other-worlds and friends long gone. And suddenly he knew what to do.

"Let's go to thirty-one meters. Let's see what's there." He kicked harder and pulled ahead. "Race you, Fundra!"

Bilk's twin sister Nikola was there waiting for them.

And she told them it was time to go home.

*

Bilk and Fundra unfolded and slipped over the sand on Thetis, but not without changing, returning to their real forms, the lumpy dry suit clinging to his body. He dropped his helmet in the surf. Fundra sent all forty-eight tips over his body, checking his health, and it seemed to Bilk that twelve of them—six on each side—danced in the air, feeling for a long trail of invisible shapes, something he'd never seen her do before.

Fundra's words came out charged, snapping around this new experience, this new array of answers. "Wings and sisters and reasons why. This is unexpected. You have power beyond me, Bilk Gib-Letton."

He stretched, yawning as if he'd just slipped out of a long night's sleep, liking the pull of morning on his muscles. "You say the funniest things. Beyond you?" He laughed, letting one hand glide along Fundra's body, following the distorted reflections of his face in her shiny rolling surface. He saw six of himself mirrored in her, all with the same stupidly comical, astonished face. He stretched his mouth into a wider grin, but only one of the reflections followed his change, and the expression died. He blinked, returned to Fundra's statement, and whispered, "Your kind, Fundra, are so far beyond us. We'd still be bound to Earth without you."

"You answered our call."

Bilk opened his hands, curling his fingers as if holding something with a strange non-uniform shape. He glanced at his reflection again and saw the shape in his mirrored hands, conjured out of his imagination. "You do things with nature that we don't comprehend. You fold things inside themselves, and unfold them when you need them. Fundra, you have non-symmetric seventeen-sided shapes that we examine without conclusion—to the end of our abilities. We can't unfold them. We can't determine their purposes. The shape could open into a full-grown flowering plum tree. It could open into a city with a kilo high vertical and a pop zone and cap of ten million inhabitants. We have eyes. We just can't see it." He expanded his gesture to the reach of his arms, ignoring the reflection of the city unfolding between his hands. "And there is nothing in the form, in the mass, in any perceptible aspect of the shape that—to us—determines its function." He repeated something his father always said about Fundra's kind. "It's like you have access to other worlds in everything you touch." He held up one hand to hold off her response. "And I'm not even talking about your sophisticated tech. This is trivial everyday use stuff that children among you can operate." Bilk shook his head as if to be certain there was nothing loose inside. "And you think I'm beyond you?"

It took Fundra a few moments, but she managed a heavy sigh —very human. "I do not believe you understand. We invited you here, my friend Bilk, to find the answer to your kind." She sent a handful of stringy appendages sweeping the sky. "We invited you across a hundred planets. We gave you the maps and means to communicate in methods suitable for you. And you have just given me a glimpse of the answer to what makes you what you are. You have shown me a world of your own making, and given me many more questions. You told me, 'We are here because I lost my sister. My parents had to get away from everything.' It is almost as if ..." She stopped to shape the words. "Almost as if you can grow like a tree without roots—or without remembering your roots. Running away from a world, leaving it out of your memory and moving on as if there was no before. That is a strange idea to me—to us. It is an ability we would like to understand. You create and shed whole worlds. You build them, and leave them behind. In all our encounters with life in the Greatest Ocean, you are the most private and sorrowful ... and world-full life we have encountered."

Bilk laughed sadly. "We can do some pretty nasty things, too. You know our history. What we're capable of?"

She dismissed his objection. "We measure you by your interest in growth, in your ability to understand, by the worlds you want to create, not in your capacity to destroy." Fundra made a shrugging motion, a roll of waves like shoulders. "Destruction is simple. Growth is difficult—understanding why things need to grow is the most difficult of all. Thetis is what it is because you are here. Earth is what it is because you are there. A hundred worlds are what they are because you have settled on them and brought your love of growth."

Bilk shifted his focus to the pale sun-flowing shape of his sister, and then along to the five copies of himself in the reflection off Fundra's surface. Apparently everyone had followed him to Thetis. Were they permanently attached to him? Were his memories real in a way he had never known? There was a sense of all five copies of himself being parts of a whole, and he could act for them all. Then there was the ghostly reflection of his sister Nikola, who was there but not part of him. She was there ... like she was *there*. And how did that happen? Bilk had always had questions for answer-seeking Fundra, but now that's all he seemed to have. Questions.

"I don't have any more answers," he whispered.

Fundra smiled at him, a rippling glow in her depths. "I think that's because it is my turn to have some for you."

Bilk frowned, and looking over Fundra, not far up the beach, he saw his mother and father and a bunch of others, a couple of the colony reps, gathered with Fundra's family. All at once the adults turned and ran or washed down the beach toward them.

Fundra's tone changed, her words coming quicker, as if she only had a short time to explain things before more formal interactive constraints would be lowered on them. "You have your twin sister."

Bilk tried to re-word her statement into something he understood. "I carry everything she meant to me?"

"You carry everything that made her your sister—with access to everything she is and was, and you carry it in your world …" Fundra fanned a dozen tips over his head. "You brought her together. The Greatest Ocean holds all things, not only memories, but the substance of the things in it at all points in time. Touch that idea with your thought, Bilk, and see your sister. It is your world. It is right to put in it the things dear to you."

Bilk turned, still trying to comprehend that, and then his mother cried out, cutting through his thoughts, and grabbed him. "Two days, Bilk? Where have you been?"

"I knew you'd come back," said Gustav, but gave Bilk a playful swat on the shoulder anyway. He pulled a lemon from his pack, the size of both his fists clasped together, and handed it to Fundra.

The col-reps were taking voice notes and nodding approvingly. The Hubery family looked disappointed for some reason.

Fundra's father, eyeing the lemon as if it was an egregious breach of etiquette, did not look pleased, turning his feelings on his daughter. "Give me everything of yours, the thunderbird, all of the things you have tipped from Bilk's memories. Until you do not fail in your responsibilities, you are no longer permitted to see Bilk."

Fundra swayed back defiantly, tips tucking in. "I did not create the lost world. Bilk did. He has all the ability and components. He just needed to be shown how to assemble them."

Bilk gave Fundra's father an open-handed gesture. "She came with me to protect me."

Fundra copied his gesture. "He made tears, and I didn't understand his purpose at first. I thought he was going to create a world for me, one in which his dead sister still lived. I didn't know it was possible, but I helped him anyway, and he ... did it. He made one. We went to a place created from his control of materials, his ideas, his perceptions. His world."

Her father made a confusing gesture, throwing water everywhere, and the expression he gave his daughter took a minute for Bilk to understand. There was a strong show of disbelief mixed with a flurry of signatures: doubt, a thin current of fear, a long chain of patterns that meant something like physical impossibility and tied in biological capabilities and limitations, culture, physiological incompatibility. Then there was revelation. "But with so few ... tips?"

"Bilk solved that as well. He has grown five of himself—five copies of Bilk." She blended a hundred strands into one reflective sheet that sent the light of Thetis' star through the near transparent copies of her human friend, arranged foot-to-foot and hand-to-hand like an unfolded paper cutout of Bilk-shaped patterns.

Fundra's father spent a moment studying Bilk. "An interesting path." He noticed with a two-tip prod the girl standing next to Bilk in the reflection, but didn't comment on her.

"Five of him grown off the original, using each finger as a tip, producing sixty. In this way, he can be considered elder to me."

Bilk looked up and into the vast and wise ocean eyes of Fundra's father. One side of Bilk's mouth curled into half a smile. "Fundra helped me. Don't take anything away from her. She has taught me so much, how to find what we have lost, how to feel the motion of the tides. How deep the water is in every one of our tears."

"Bilk has answered." Fundra said solemnly, folding three long tendrils over Bilk's shoulders. "He has given us more than we were seeking. Our journey is never complete, but in this one regard, it is over."

Bilk looked around, from his parents to Fundra's father, and then up to Fundra. "Over?" He pointed out the tides. "Tomorrow's always a new day with new things to learn, new things to teach."

Fundra made her very human sounding laugh, holding up Gustav's gift. "That is so. And still many old things." She held up Gustav's gift. "Lemons. Your father's warm fingers curled around the seedling of a lemon tree. Try to find that across the Greatest Ocean." She paused only a moment. "I will spare you the challenge. You will not find it outside yourselves and a few other kinds." Fundra held up all forty-eight of her tips, her full fan. "We have looked. We have tipped whole worlds for others who have—as you say, climbed far. If they exist, they have not heard our call."

Fundra's father made a rolling motion that everyone understood to mean he was intrigued by this change, that he was sur-prised by its apparent depth, and he would have to spend a long time thinking about it. He bowed to Jovita and Gustav, curled up and stabbed nineteen tips, nine of them fanned into the air, the others at the waves, directing his accompanying oceanfarers away.

And Bilk took that to mean that he and Fundra were off the hook—everyone's hooks. "See you tomorrow, Fundra?"

She made a gesture with almost all of her tips, the rest of them still holding the bright yellow lemon. "Yes, you will."

He took his mother's and father's hands, gave them each a squeeze, and then let them go. "I have one more thing to tell you." Bilk pointed to his head. "I found Nikola. She was in here and across the universe—the Greatest Ocean—the whole time, wait-ing to get out, waiting to come back together. Maybe we tried to leave her at Home. But she followed us here."

Bilk looked up on the last few words, smiled, following the curve of sand to his sister who had run ahead. Nikola stopped with the starlight shining through her and turned, smiling back at him, her feet sinking in the seawater that played at the edge of their new world.

There was a promise in her smile, that she would be there to-morrow.

***

Chris Howard is a creative guy with a pen and a paint brush, author of Seaborn *(Juno Books),* Salvage *(Masque, 2013),* Nanowhere, *and a shelf-full of other books. His short stories have appeared in a bunch of magazines and antholo-gies, including "Lost Dogs and Fireplace Archeology" in*

Fantasy Magazine. *His story "Hammers and Snails" was a* Robert A. Heinlein Centennial Short Fiction Contest *winner. He writes and illustrates the comic,* Saltwater Witch. *His ink work and digital illustrations have appeared in* Shimmer, BuzzyMag, *various RPGs, and on the pages and covers of books, blogs, and other interesting places. Last year he painted a 9 x 12 foot Steampunk Map of New York for a cafe in Brooklyn. Find out everything at* http://www.SaltwaterWitch.com

Afterword

I am in awe of this anthology. Not just of the stories, and they are indeed fine stories, but of the shared road traveled by the stories' authors. Mark their names, because you'll be seeing a lot more of them.

Some years ago, when Craig Shaw Gardner suggested to me that perhaps we should run a workshop for aspiring science fiction and fantasy writers, I agreed without too much hesitation. We had both taught at workshops before—Odyssey, New England Young Writers Conference, and others—and we both enjoyed working with other writers. In fact, we have been part of the same local writing group (called, cleverly, "the writing group") for over thirty years! So, committed, we secured some meeting space at the Pandemonium bookstore in Cambridge, Massachusetts, called ourselves the Ultimate SF Writing Workshop, and put out some flyers.

We had a pretty good idea of what to expect, and we got that and more: students with huge imaginations, and wildly varying degrees of talent and craft. Often enough, at the beginning, the talent and imagination outstripped the skills of the writers. And that was perfect for a workshop. I don't think you can teach talent,

195

though sometimes you can tease imagination out of a mind that just needs the right trigger. But craft and skill—those you can work with, and develop, and watch grow. And that's what we set out to do, although truthfully, Craig and I didn't so much teach as help these new writers learn from each other.

And learn and grow they did! Over the course of several years of the workshop, including some advanced sessions for the most motivated, we saw nascent talent blossom into professionalism. We followed with pleasure as alumni members sold stories to magazines, published novels, and in a few cases went on to participate in other professional-quality workshops, like Odyssey and Viable Paradise. We all stayed in touch, through a continuing online group and regular meet-ups at local conventions. It was at one such meet-up, a dinner at Readercon, that the idea for this anthology was born.

Two things I didn't expect when we started the workshops:

One, that Craig and I would learn so much from the students, and that working with them would inspire our own writing. Two, that we would come out of it with a roomful of new friends and colleagues to join us in our battle to try to take over the world, *literarily* speaking.

No, there's a third thing I didn't expect—that so much damn fine writing would come out of it, just few years later. The contents of this book are just a sample. I should add that Craig and I are, I guess you could say, benevolent godfathers to this anthology. We gave it our blessing and our best wishes, but all of the work was done by the workshop alums, from the selection and editing of the stories, right down to the cover art and the formatting and book design. I'm mighty pleased to be associated with it, even if I didn't lift a finger to create it myself.

I said it before, but it's worth repeating:

Remember the names of these authors—KJ Kabza, William Gerke, Julia Rios, Timothy S. Kroecker, E.L. Mellor, Meredith Watts, Talib S. Hussain, Scott Davis, Fernando Salazar, LJ Cohen, and Chris Howard—because you're going to see lots of good things coming from them. I guarantee it.

—Jeffrey A. Carver
July 2013

Acknowledgments

This anthology is a reality because of the dedication, hard work, and patience of all the authors whose work resides between its covers. One year ago, at Readercon 2012, a group of local writers, all graduates from various years of Jeff Carver's and Craig Shaw Gardner's Ultimate SF Writing Workshop, had a reunion dinner. From a conversation at that large table, the seeds for this anthology project were sown.

In the past year, we have worked together to honor the workshop model, employing peer review, critique, and revision in order to create *Pen-Ultimate*.

From the start, we decided to donate 100% of the proceeds from *Pen-Ultimate's* sales to the Science Fiction and Fantasy Writers of America's (SFWA) emergency medical fund. This fund offers interest-free loans to SFWA members facing unexpected medical expenses. We hope you will enjoy reading our stories as you support an important cause.

Lisa (LJ) would like to thank her co-editor, Talib S. Hussain, for his patience and for dealing with a control freak with such grace. She would also like to give a special shout out to Chris Howard for the fabulous cover and to Mary Ann Marcinkiewicz for copy-editing in the eleventh hour. And Lisa is grateful for Jeff and Craig's support, guidance, and friendship.

Talib would like to thank Jeff and Craig not only for their valuable workshops in which he learned a LOT, but also for their continued efforts to ensure that all graduates from their workshops stay in touch and share their ideas and progress. He would also like to thank Lisa, who had the initial inspiring thought that sparked the first anthology conversation and for many fun collaborative discussions as we reviewed stories and process (she's not really a control freak ...).

Lisa Janice (LJ) Cohen
Talib S. Hussain
July 2013